Dark Waters

Vol. 2

Dark Waters

Vol. 2

Contents

For a list of trigger warnings, please see pg 207

A note from the editors

The Dark Waters team is as shocked as you that we're still here, still kicking, and releasing our second anthology.

To everyone that's supported us, and to everyone new who this might reach, we offer our sincere thanks.

We dedicate this to all who believe dark fiction exists in dark times, now more than ever.

Best,
Nate & Kirstyn

Road Work

R.D. Sullivan

"Shit," Brent said as he rounded the corner and spotted the flagger standing under a circle of light. He shot a nervous glance at the girl next to him— Cara or Klara or Kiara—but she was still curled into a ball on the passenger seat. He tugged her skirt down over her ass and slowed the Corvette.

They'd passed a "Road Work Ahead" sign half a mile back and he'd hoped it was just a forgotten bit of detritus from construction past. No such luck, but they were within ten miles of his cabin. He just had to get through this, get there, and then the fun could begin.

Everything would work out.

He gave his most charming smile as the flagger walked to his window.

She wore gold-rimmed aviators beneath a white hard hat, curly brown locks tumbling out from her ponytail. Under her orange vest was a set of denim bibs over a tank top, allowing for just a hint of an impressive rack. Her lips were painted a shade of red unfit for working a road crew in the middle of the night.

But he knew the odds were good that as killer as she looked at first glance, something was deeply fucked up about this woman. Missing teeth, skin sores, stretch marks… Hard to say without getting her undressed.

And like hell he was going to approach that. This bitch wasn't flagging traffic at night because she had her shit together.

"Nice car!" she said, proving him wrong about the missing teeth. Hers were straight and bright white as she grinned. "Is this the Z06? Damn, must be—"

"It is," he said, cutting her off. He wanted her away from his window and out of his business, not making chit-chat to pass the time. "What's going on?"

"Not a whole lot, what's going on with you?"

If he was a religious man, he'd be praying to the patron saint of stupid conversations right now.

"No. What's up with the…" He gestured towards the light plant, its diesel engine chugging happily along, and at the three cones set up across his lane.

She laughed. "I know, I know. There was a rockslide, so we're having to run a pilot car until they can get equipment up here to clear it. Shouldn't be long, maybe…" She trailed off and looked up the road.

The poor thing, Brent thought. You can see both her brain cells trying to find each other in there.

"…probably about ten minutes. You just missed the car leaving, but it's not a long stretch. Should be back soon—"

"Ten minutes?" he asked. It popped out unbidden,

incredulous. The woman looked taken aback. That pearly white smile faltered.

"Probably less," she offered. Hedging.

He sucked his teeth in annoyance. It's why women never got anywhere. Too easy to bully. Too quick to hem and haw and offer appeasements.

Cara or Klara or Kiara whimpered next to him, clutching her stomach and curling into a tighter ball in the seat.

The woman frowned. "Hey man, is your daughter okay?"

His irritation must have flashed across his face because the bitch at his window took a step back, raising one hand in surrender.

He loved nothing more than a scared woman. Her reaction made his blood shift southward, and he looked at the girl next to him and licked his lips before he could stop himself.

"Look, I'm sorry, I was just—"

"She's fine," he snapped. "Just tired and sitting here isn't helping us get home."

He didn't correct her on the daughter part. She didn't need to know.

"Look, I get it," the lady said. She stood upright, still backed away from his window, and twisted back and forth to stretch her back. "It'll only be a few more minutes. You all live out here?"

"I have a cabin up the road."

Short. Curt. Unfriendly. Everyone at his company knew that tone and knew not to press, yet here was this dumb cunt, back in his window with that stupid grin on her face.

"Oh man, that's gotta be great! Nice and secluded. No neighbors." She looked at him over the top of her glasses. "Nobody to hear you scream."

Brent stiffened and shot another look at the girl. He'd said those very words, countless times, to his guests, yet to hear it

rolling so easily off
the tongue of this
stranger shot a chill
through his veins.

And then she was laughing, even reaching through the window to lightly shove his arm.

"Ho boy, you should have seen your face! I'm kidding, I'm kidding, couldn't help myself. I'm a huge—"

A huge what, he never found out. She stood and looked as lights came around the corner behind them. A giant diesel truck slowed and rumbled to a stop seemingly inches from his bumper. The jackass sat there a good thirty seconds with their brights on before they hit the dimmer, but the damage was done. Not just to his night vision, but his mood as well.

At least it got the dumb bitch's attention.

"Be right back," she said, eyeing the truck. "Better let them know what's up."

Once she was gone, Brent groaned and squeezed the leather steering wheel until it creaked. He'd been coming up here like this for years. Not once had he slowed down for so much as a damn possum crossing the road. Yet here now he sat, cross-examined by some broad who couldn't mind her own damn business, waiting for a fucking car because they assumed he was too stupid to drive around rocks.

Sure, sometimes the trip back to the city was rough, when the girls wouldn't stop crying, or trying to wound him with verbal arrows. Never on the way out, though.

Static cut through the night, followed by a garbled voice. He watched the flagger pull a radio from her bibs and answer, then listen to the response. He hadn't known she had a radio on her, but he figured she could hide damn near anything in that get-up.

It wasn't until she started walking back to his window that he realized he'd forgotten to roll it up.

"Pilot car should be… There it is." She pointed ahead and he spotted the lights as they flashed between trees, maybe a half mile out.

The girl gave another whimper, nearly a small cry.

"You sure she's okay?" The damn flagger was back leaning on his car, head in the open window. "I've got some extra water, I can bring her—"

"She's. Fine." He said it with his boardroom finality, a practiced combination of condescension and conclusion.

"Whatever," the woman muttered. "Your funeral."

And yet, she didn't move. Just kept her forearm against his car, getting her blue-collar greasy skin on his pristine paint job.

He wanted to shove her away but clenched his fists instead.

Just a few more seconds. The pilot car was almost here, it'd turn around, and he'd be safely on his way. No point in making a scene that would get him remembered.

They both watched the pilot car come around the last bend, but his relief turned to anger as, instead of flipping around to lead him through, it nosed up to his car and stopped moving.

"What the fuck are they doing?" he demanded. He gestured at the driver to turn around, but they didn't move. His mood was slowly souring from annoyed to apoplectic, the only solace that he had a hot piece to take it out on later.

A hot piece, who picked this moment to groan, sit up, look at him, and whimper, "Take me home, mister."

It caught him so off-guard that he stared at her instead of noticing the flagger drop her stop sign and reach back into her bibs. He was just turning back to her, already crafting the lie about his drunk daughter, when she pressed the metal barrel of a gun into his temple.

There was no helping it. He froze. Hands hovered, shaking over the steering wheel as he stuttered a surprised "Wha-wha-what?"

She sighed and pulled her glasses off. The eyes behind them were bright, alert, and, most shockingly of all, two different colors. One was a pale blue and the other a deep brown.

The word heterochromatic popped unbidden into his mind. Not a word he'd normally store but, he realized as his throat went dry and his asshole clenched in fear, that he'd seen a matching pair.

Recently.

"It's genetic," the girl a couple of months ago had said. "My older sister has a matching set."

This woman had an assurance about her the younger one had lacked and was old enough to be out of his target range.

He had to assume this was the sister.

Suddenly, Brent wanted to puke.

"You okay, Elise?" the woman, the sister, asked.

It made his brain seize up, the question making little sense, until the girl next to him—previously Cara or whatever—popped upright and leaned across him to grin up out of the window, sober and bright-eyed.

Brent's hands shook and he licked his lips nervously.

"Right as rain!" the girl said. "But I can't open my door from this side. Like a trap."

"You sneaky fuck," the woman with the gun said, accentuating each word with a jab into his temple. "Amanda!" she shouted to the truck behind him. "Open the passenger door and let Elise out!"

A truck door slammed and moments later, his date was steadily exiting his car.

"This isn't what… It's not… I was just trying to…"

She scoffed at all his false starts. "I saw what you were just trying to do when you sent the video of it to my sister. I read the threats to send it to her family, her boss, and the college dean if she kept making noise. I know exactly what you were just trying to do."

The woman slammed a fist into the top of the Corvette and Brent, despite it all, winced for the car. Let these cunts have their little revenge play but for fuck's sake, the car was only a couple months off the lot.

"Elise, collapse the light plant like I showed you. You remember where we're meeting? Good. Take the truck there and wait. Chelsea, Tara—stay there until I get fuckwit moved, then we'll get out of here before anyone shows up." She leaned back down, forearm on his windowsill, and gestured at the passenger seat with the gun. "Slide over, fuckwit."

Brent stared at her in disbelief a long moment before his brain clicked back on. Like hell, he thought. No way and no how was he going to let this dumb bitch take his car, not to mention himself, away from this road.

She'd just opened her mouth to run it more when he grabbed the clutch, threw it in reverse, and stomped on the gas.

For the foot the car moved, he felt victorious. Then there was a hard crunch and he was thrown back hard against his seat.

The truck behind him. He'd forgotten about the damn truck behind him.

No matter. Maybe it bought him enough space to go forward and—

The pilot car rolled forward and his Corvette jumped again as the bumpers met.

The Corvette stalled and he looked around wildly for the gun-wielding psycho. He'd expected her to follow but she stood where he'd left her, hand on her hip, looking amused of all things.

It was terrifying.

The pilot car hit their brights, and the truck behind him followed suit. He was trapped in a blinding wall of light and he twisted to get away from it, only to see the woman in the orange vest walking towards his car.

Fight or flight hit him. Blood sank to his legs and it felt as if the bottom of his stomach fell away. He scrambled for the controls, rolling up his window and slapping at the panel until the locks clicked home.

If he could just hold out, maybe another car would come along—hell, maybe even a cop!—and see what was happening, arrest these women, and save—

Tap

Tap

Tap

The woman in the vest rapped the gun barrel against his window. When he turned her way, she grinned and waved.

"Fuck off!" he yelled.

Maybe the passenger door? Maybe he could just get out, run into the woods, and let her—

A second woman stepped into view outside of the passenger door. This one wore tight black pants and a black tank top. She had long, glossy black hair that swayed as she lowered her face to his window.

And stared. Not moving. No threat. Just stood, stared, and let it be known he wasn't getting out that way either.

Brent's hands felt weak. He couldn't drive. Couldn't run. And that whore with the gun was tapping steadily on the glass with the barrel.

Tap

Tap

Tap

Jaw clenched, hands white-knuckled on the steering wheel, he forced himself to look her way.

She arched an eyebrow and held up three fingers.

Brent shook his head, not understanding. Until she lowered the first finger. She cocked her head to see if he understood now and started to lower the second finger.

He dove for the window control. The moment the glass was down, she pressed the barrel back against his head.

"Scoot. Over." She said.

This time he scrambled to comply, knocking his knees into the gear shift and the console in his haste. She slid into the seat he'd vacated and tucked the pistol under her left thigh.

Away from him.

The knock on the window next to his head made him yelp in surprise, and the woman in his car chuckled softly as she rolled his window down.

The black-clad woman on the passenger side of the car grabbed his chin, digging her nails in as she turned his face towards her.

"We'll be ahead of and behind you. Try anything and we'll break your legs and haul you into the forest to die."

The woman in his car laughed.

"Wow. Dark, Bianca."

The woman, Bianca, let go of his face and shrugged. "Kisses.

Be careful."

"Who are you all?" he demanded as the woman started his car.

She thought about it for a moment before turning to him.

"Angry. We're angry."

‡

They drove in silence. The pilot car led the way and every time he checked the mirror, the pickup was a few lengths behind. The woman driving hummed to herself and drummed on the steering wheel, pausing only to shift around tight turns.

Brent wanted to believe his nausea was motion sickness, but it was a hard sell when he'd never actually had it before. No, his sphincter-clenching cold sweats hit a little harder every time he thought of her last words: "We're angry."

The ease with which they'd backed him into a corner, forced his compliance, was terrifying. He'd lost all control in a matter of minutes, gone from massaging that hot little slut's bare ass to feeling his balls running for the safety of his gut. None of them had said what was planned for him, but he couldn't leave it to chance. They'd made no demands, but maybe they hadn't known what he could offer.

Maybe they underestimated who they were dealing with.

Pulling everything he'd learned about negotiating from the recesses of his mind, he crossed his arms and cleared his throat.

"Don't ride the clutch like that."

Opening volley. Unbalance her.

But she just laughed softly again and shifted smoothly coming out of a corner.

"I'm a very wealthy man, you know," he said as she resumed humming. "Whatever you ladies want I can get it in a couple hours, by morning, tops. Six, seven figures. You name it."

The woman turned briefly to smile at him, but it was without joy, without humor. It held bitterness and cruelty and made his stomach lurch.

"We're ladies now, Trent?"

"Brent!" he said before he could stop himself.

"Not whores, cunts, bitches, sluts, life support for our holes, like you said in the video?"

"I… I didn't mean… I don't know what—"

"Or is that talk reserved for just your sexy fun times?" She gave him one last measured look, before turning her eyes back to the road.

Suddenly his throat was paper-dry and he had to jam his fists in his lap to stop their shaking. Money ruled his world. No sane person could be offered a million bucks and not even consider it.

Which meant he wasn't dealing with sane people.

"Stop the car and let me out now and I won't press charges."

She didn't slow, didn't even look.

"Let me out!" he screamed, and all she did was arch an eyebrow at him.

The panic he'd kept a lid on up until now burst free. Wherever these cunts were taking him, he doubted it was for a long chat and a handshake. Steeling himself for the pain, telling himself to roll, he lunged for the handle and chucked his body weight against the door.

Pain shot through his shoulder as it hit unyielding glass and upholstery. The door didn't so much as click, the handle as useful as a limp fish in his fist.

"You disabled the latch, remember?" she said. His fit hadn't even phased her. He was still trapped in this car with this psycho bitch being taken to God only knew where.

Letting it happen was not an option.

"Let me out!" he screamed again, and dove for her.

She was quicker. Grabbing the clutch and the brake, she put the car in a smooth skid, sending him flying forward. Something popped in his chest as it hit the dash and when his head hit the windshield, darkness stole him away.

‡

"Wakey-wakey, sleepy head!" a voice sing-songed.

Brent was confused. His head throbbed. He felt like he was in motion and crammed someplace small. Every breath made his chest hurt. It was a fight to rise back to consciousness and he groaned with the effort.

"There he is," the voice said. A heavy palm landed on his cheek, the sting of it pulling him closer to the surface.

Close enough he started to remember. The panic hit quick and he began to fight the constriction around him. The binds were unyielding but he fought, even as he realized he was half crammed on the floorboards.

"Easy, tiger," she said.

She. That cunt with the eyes. Driving his car. He wanted to strangle her but pulling himself up into his seat left him dizzy, winded, and feeling like he had a knife in his chest.

The car slowed and she followed the pilot car in a hard left off the highway, past an all-too-familiar mailbox and up an all-too-familiar gravel drive.

"What…" he mumbled. "How…" The words were sticky in his cotton mouth, and she didn't look interested in answering anyway. But of all the places he thought they'd take him, his own house hadn't made the list.

The moment the car was in the garage, the gun was back in

her hand. If there'd been an opportunity, he'd missed it, but he couldn't even tell through his damn headache.

"Now behave," she said, then cocked her head. "Or what is it you say on the videos? 'Or fight me. I like it when you fight me'?"

Brent glared, but those icy, mismatched eyes stayed unfazed. He wanted to argue, shout back, defend himself, but there was nothing he could say to having his own words regurgitated at him.

He jumped when his door opened.

"Step out slow," the black-clad woman, Bianca, said from behind him.

His driver smirked. "Best do it. We don't agree on the plan, she doesn't think it's enough for you."

"What plan?" he asked, hating the fear he could hear in his own voice. "Enough what?"

"Violence," she said with a grin, and got out of the car.

‡

They marched him through his own cabin, two women leading the way and the other three behind, gun to his back. A part of him almost hoped they'd be distracted by the worth of the place; show an interest in robbing him blind. If they cared about money, he could…

But no. They didn't even take in the high ceilings, the crystal decanter, the art. The ones in front went straight for the stairs, and the ones behind pushed him on in their wake.

Upstairs, they didn't go for the jewelry box, or even look at the safe. They forced him into his bedroom, stopped next to his bed, and someone kicked his knees out from under him.

The five stood around him, kneeling on the carpet like a supplicant before them. Five angry, glaring faces, eyes only for him.

But everybody has a price.

"I'm rich," he tried. The girl with the gun was a no-go, but the other…maybe. "I can get you however much you want. I can have cash delivered here and we can pretend this never happened. I can—"

"You can shut the fuck up," said Bianca and made as if to slap him.

Brent flinched, and instantly felt his face go red-hot as a small laugh went up around the circle.

"Not so tough now, are you?" one behind him, a short brunette with killer curves asked.

Not that he could answer, now that the gun was back against his head.

"Where do you keep them?" the woman with two-toned eyes asked.

"What?" he asked.

She sighed and dropped the gun to her side. "Now is not the time to fuck around. You know what we want. Where are they?"

He tried to look at the other women, a desperate plea for help, but they all just continued to glare.

"I don't know! I don't know what you're looking for!"

"The hard way then."

He didn't have time to wonder what she meant by "the hard way" as his entire body seized and all he knew was pain. A scream tried to tear its way through clenched teeth and his brain felt close to melting and running from his ears.

Then, as quickly as it had started, it was over. The switch on the fire hose of agony was flipped off and he lay, face against the carpet, panting. One side of his crotch and hip were soaked.

He'd pissed himself.

Insult to injury, that horrible cunt was crouching in front of him, gently caressing his cheek and shushing him.

"Shh, big guy, don't be embarrassed. Sometimes the girls probably wet themselves too, huh? Now…" She stood and used one booted foot to roll him onto his back.

He saw the taser in the hand of a blonde with an athletic build. One who'd be pretty, if she didn't have so much spite in her eyes.

"…Where are they?" the cunt asked again.

Brent had to stammer his answer through jagged, rapid breaths. "I… I don't… What are you looking for?"

"Shame," she said, and shot her chin at the blond. "Do him again."

"No!" he screamed. "Wait! I—"

Wait she did not, digging the prongs into his side and tearing his world apart with pain once more.

"What was that?" the leader asked him again as the agony receded. "Did I hear a change of heart?"

"Closet," he wheezed. Jesus, was he having a heart attack? Or just a taser on a likely broken rib? "This closet. Attic access, up there. Ladder in the hallway closet."

He squeezed his eyes shut as two of the women split off without a word, one to his closet and one to the hallway.

Fingers trailed through his hair as the ringleader *tsked* softly, once more crouching over him.

"I know, I know. It's awful being helpless at the hands of someone who means you harm, huh? Imagine how all the girls felt. And we aren't even going to fuck you."

"I have money," he said, chin trembling as he spoke. "Lots. Lots of money. Whatever you want, we can—"

"Found it!" one of the women called from the walk-in closet.

"We know you have money. That's why it has to be this way." She gave his cheek one last pat. "Bring it all out!" she called to the two in the closet. "Put it on the bed. And you. Get up slowly and face the bed."

"I'm sorry. I'm so sorry." He brought his hands up, palms out, as if presenting his remorse to the women. "I have a sickness, I'm not right. I'll donate everything I have, I'll make up for it and get help, I—"

The taser bit into his side and Brent screamed. He screamed just like the girls who he'd told that nobody would hear them.

‡

He stood, thighs against the mattress, staring at the pile on the foot of his bed. DVDs. Memory cards. External hard drives. Polaroids. The bits and bobs of their jewelry or items from their purse he kept for souvenirs. A remnant of every girl he'd brought here since he'd bought the cabin a decade ago.

Along with everything else he kept on hand.

Lube. Condoms. Rope. Gags.

His video camera.

All of his sins, out in the open for these women to see and judge.

Except for the handcuffs. Their leader had taken those and was busy cinching them tight—too tight—around his wrists.

Shameful, pain-extorted tears wet his cheeks at the sight of the pile.

"Please," he whispered. "I'm sorry. Just tell me what you want and I'll do it. Anything. Name it."

"What I want," the woman said, and spun him to face her, "is for you to take this experience away from my sister. From all those women." She pointed at the pile on the bed, face cold with fury. No levity, no joviality was left in either eye, just spite and anger. "To give them back their sense of safety and peace of mind."

"Prison is too good for you," said another woman, the blond with the taser.

"You'll just wind up in Club Fed and be out in a couple years." The black-clad one. Bianca.

"I'll… I'll…" he sputtered. "I'm sorry." He was blubbering and couldn't stop himself.

"You're only sorry you got caught," said the woman with two different eyes. "Get on the bed. Hands to the eye bolt. Don't pretend it's not there, either."

He opened his mouth to protest, remembered the taser, and shut it. Knees shaking, he crawled across the bed to the pillows. Once his back was against the wall, he sought out the eye bolt with his fingers, handcuffs clinking against it.

The leader pressed his shoulder forward and reached behind him. A click, then she stood back, watching. His grasping fingers trailed along a long U of cold metal, joined by a square.

A padlock. They'd padlocked him to the wall.

He'd had the eye bolt installed special.

It wasn't coming out.

All five women stared at him, handcuffed and locked to the wall.

"Are you all sure?" the leader asked quietly.

They all seriously considered it before nodding, none taking their eyes off him.

"Then let's get to it."

Another heartbeat of the cold stares before they turned and went downstairs.

"Please!" he yelled at their backs. "You can't leave me here like this! It's torture!"

Only retreating footsteps on the stairs, and shuffling downstairs.

"Please!" he shrieked in panic. "I'm sorry!"

The front door slammed, the garage door rumbled, and Brent had to fight to breathe.

"It'll be okay," he told himself. "It'll be okay."

Would it? How long would it be until someone found him?

Monday, he suddenly remembered, and he could have cried with relief.

Most of the time he fucked up, so excited for a trip to his cabin with a guest star that he forgot to book the cleaners until the following week, but he'd remembered this time.

Monday.

They would be here to clean Monday.

It was, what? Early Saturday morning? That meant only two days to survive here, handcuffed to the bed.

He could tell them it was a date gone wrong. They didn't have to know what was on the memory sticks and hard drives. A pile of extra cash, some assurances, and they wouldn't breathe word one to anyone.

And then he'd find out who those dumb whores were and he'd—

An ear-spitting shrill shot through the quiet of his cabin and he flinched. Jesus, what a time for the smoke detector to go off. He could survive without food and water but listening to that might—

A second shrieking joined the first, off-beat and discordant.

The first was downstairs but the new sound was coming from the one mounted in the upstairs hallway.

Sniffing experimentally, he leaned forward as if that would let him know faster. Nothing at first, and then…

Brent's balls crawled so far up his stomach they were making friends with his gallbladder.

His house was filling with smoke. Visible tendrils of it crested the stairs and began curling their way toward the bedrooms.

They'd handcuffed him to his bed and lit his house on fire.

Panic threw out any sense he had left and sent him bucking and twisting against the cuffs. He yanked at the eye bolt even as his skin gave, even as his bones bruised, because anything would be better than burning alive in his own bed.

But he'd had the eye bolt installed special.

It wasn't going anywhere.

R.D. Sullivan is a writer of fiction, comedy and letters to the editor. She lives in North Carolina with one good kid and two bad dogs. Her writing has been featured at Fireside Fiction Magazine, Rock and a Hard Place Press, Shotgun Honey, and Tough, as well as in numerous anthologies, including one devoted entirely to ham sandwiches in which she published an erotic story. She also authored the novella *Hotties and Bazingas and the Murder Cult Murders* which she will only discuss over whiskey. You can track her down at govneh.com.

Her grandmother would like you to know she is the source of all RD's talent.

Animal Remains

Mary Thorson

West Virginia, 1946

People felt funny about the Knotty Pine Rest Stop, especially after Sylvia's father was found dead on the side of the road. But Sylvia knew it started before that. Near the end, her father started to manically collect and pile things on the shelves before he died. She remembered the way his mind went. He'd cut out ads for estate sales like other people cut coupons and mark maps with routes up and down the highway so he could get to as many as possible in one day. They'd close down the rest stop at odd times and people got frustrated. The things he would pick up made no sense to Sylvia, and she didn't ask because she was afraid of him. He gathered other people's messes in bulk and stored them without order, keeping the mess intact. Customers stopped staying to eat as the mess overflowed into the dining area. Taxidermy, pictures of other people's families, cigar boxes, signs for other places cluttered the window. Sylvia knew none of it was for sale.

She was there when he walked out of the store and into the road. She must have heard the little bell ring over the door as he went out. She didn't notice it. She was in the back room staring at the newest box he'd brought in, steeling herself before she would have to open it. It was the silence she noticed. She couldn't hear his body moving through the aisles; his feet dragging up and down the linoleum floors. She went out to the front of the store and knew she was alone. She walked to the door and stared at the stuffed fox with just one eye placed like a guard dog, and then saw him outside. There was nobody out there with him, over him, waving for help—he was alone and crumpled up. Discarded. When she got closer she could see that his shoes were gone. His socks were dirty. He was a pile. He was a mess.

‡

"Have you seen us?" it said above the photograph. *"We're the Sodder Children and we went missing on Christmas Eve, 1945, when our house burned down in a fire."* The way the ad had been worded made the voice in Sylvia's head sound like a chorus of children when she read it. There they were, the five of them, each looking out at her with dark eyes. There were two boys and three girls, ordered by age. Only one of them was smiling, and only partially. Even the youngest, the toddler, looked serious. All closed mouths.

She had seen them weeks before. Only for a second, she told herself, there was no way she could be sure—but she knew it was them. Ever since Kathy had come in from outside, the first time since Sylvia's father died, all concerned about those kids in the car out there, Sylvia thought the five of them had been with her. She'd hear little things in the back of her empty store. Things that sounded so intentional. Like footsteps and breathing and once or twice, even screaming—someone very small would scream and Sylvia would run from her tiny house behind the Knotty Pine and search the aisle for a toddler with big dark eyes and find nothing. Just mess and silence.

She put away the paper and she could hear them. Loud at first, all talking at once, but then quiet when she started to drink. It was a strange sensation. Sylvia could feel their dark eyes on her when she ran her finger over the remains of strangers' things and let the dust gather up under her nail. How was she supposed to know? An ache had started in the hollow of her neck, the same place she felt her heart flutter when it fell out of rhythm. The ache spread slowly up her throat until it was at the back of her mouth. When it made its way to her tongue, she found she was grinding her teeth.

‡

"That family out there, the man is acting real strange. All

those kids are upset," Kathy said.

Sylvia had looked behind her and saw them scrunched up in the backseat with a man yelling at them to be quiet. She had seen that many times before. People pulled over when they were at the end of their rope. Tension pouring out of the open car doors. Kathy was a remnant of before, someone who would come in three times a week for cigarettes and lunch. Sylvia remembered her order: tuna melt. Now, she rarely came, and she certainly never came inside. She'd pull up outside and Sylvia would meet her at the pump.

Kathy was jumpy as Sylvia watched her glance at the little sign at the window next to the front door asking for information about what happened to her father. Every night, Sylvia willed herself to take it down, and every night she failed.

"I'm sorry, it's out of order," Sylvia lied. She didn't know why she was lying, but she didn't want this woman in her store. She was an intruder now. "Besides, it's the day after Christmas, everyone's a little rattled after the holidays. Lots of sugar and liquor to keep everyone on edge." But what she really wanted to say was you must know what happened to him. Someone knows something.

Kathy had wrung her hands together as thoughts clicked over and over and over in Sylvia's head. They both watched as the car peeled out of the station, one of the kids' big eyes staring out the rear window as she clung to the top of the backseat. Sylvia could almost make out her tiny fingers gripping into the leather. Kathy turned back around with a desperate look, then paid for her gas before she quickly left.

‡

Sylvia was sweating when George Sodder came in. She was in a booth at the very back of the store with her cheek on the table. She had drunk too much the night before, trying to summon the courage to open up one of her father's unopened boxes, but unable. She thought she could see small greasy fingerprints scattered along the edges of the cardboard. Sylvia didn't see him at first, but the bell over the door rang and she lifted her head and saw the circular stain her face had left. Underneath the table, she felt a small hand begin to wrap around her ankle and she kicked into the shadowed empty space at her feet like a child swinging their legs because they couldn't reach the floor.

She got up and walked behind the counter, and there she had a better view of him. He was frantic. He had deep lines that seemed to be cracking his face into pieces, and every movement he made was like a jerk in an unintended direction.

"I'm looking for the owner," he said, without any "hello" or "excuse me." Sylvia felt as if she had taken something from him, and she wanted to crouch down behind the counter.

"My name's Sylvia, sir," she said, though that's not what he had asked her.

She reached out her hand, and he looked at it as if she were holding out a piece of chewed gum. Then, she thought, he might grab her and drag her over the countertop. She knew he wasn't there to buy anything. She almost pulled it away when he grasped it.

"So, it was you who saw them? You saw my kids?"

"Your kids?" She knew, then, who he was.

"On Christmas. The police said you saw them here on Christmas morning." His eyes darted around as if children might start crawling out of the walls, and then they did. One by one.

George put his other hand out, flat, raising and lowering it, attempting to indicate their heights. He let go of her and rifled through his pockets. Her hand was suddenly cold and damp, and she pulled it back into herself, holding it to her chest. Everything about him made her want to shrivel down into herself and hide.

"You told the police you saw them the morning after the fire." George brought out a cutout from a newspaper and laid it flat on the counter.

It was the same notice she'd seen before. Her hand twitched, she wanted to cover them up, but it wouldn't matter. She was starting to see them all the time. Little fingers gripping shelves on the other side of the aisle she'd be stocking. Five twin lights staring at her from underneath the counters. Several children all whispering at the same time: have you seen us?

"Did you really see them? Did they…" George paused and hung his head for a moment as he used everything to catch his breath. "Did they seem alright?"

"I didn't see your children, sir," Sylvia whispered back, keeping her eyes down. She sensed a shift—a pack moving into perfect position. Coordinated, intact, dangerous.

"But you could have, or else you wouldn't have told the police," George offered.

Sylvia stared at the yellowing collar of his shirt where it cut into his neck.

Kathy must have gone to another telephone. There was a small bait shop down the road. Sylvia's father always complained that it cut into their business, but then she would remind him that nothing they sold was alive. Sylvia wondered if she mentioned her. She wouldn't even let me use the phone. Sylvia wondered if, when Kathy was telling the cops where she saw those kids, she'd said something like you know, where that man got hit and killed last year.

The bell rang as another man came in. A stranger. She fixed her eyes on this one as he walked straight towards the bathrooms, willing him to look back at her. George started to say something again, but she cut him off.

"Can I help you with anything?" she yelled across to the new guest.

He turned, confused about who she was talking to, and then kept walking to the bathroom.

"Listen," George said. "Can you just take a look, again? I've been up and down the highway trying to find which one they stopped at, trying to find you. My wife and I, we know that someone took them, see. They're not dead. Can you look, please?"

Sylvia squinted at the ad, and the dull ache in her skull grew sharper as she studied the features on their faces that she'd already seen in her peripheral vision. Things you could not miss. Thick eyebrows, black hair, and dark eyes.

"Dead?" Sylvia asked. He waved his hand in front of his face and she flinched.

"It's impossible. There's no way there'd be nothing left after only 45 minutes. It's too short a time to burn up a body." He spoke about the matter so logically, like they weren't his kids and their bodies he talked about. "My wife has been doing experiments," he whispered, leaning closer. "She can't get the bones to burn. And this is chicken and turkey bones we're talking about. She lets them go for hours, but the bones are still left. Human bones are stronger than that, and it's just not possible for there to be nothing left. She even spoke with a man who works in a crematorium—you know, where they burn the bodies after you die. He said it took at least five hours at a much higher heat than what we had at that fire."

He reached into his pocket again and brought out little, black, hard things that he scattered on the counter. "You see?" he asked, pushing them around with his fingers. They looked like charred twigs.

"Please, sir," Sylvia said. "Can you take those back?"

"Sorry," he said, sweeping them off the counter into his hand.

The person from the bathroom walked up behind George Sodder and waited. Sylvia flashed a big smile at him over George's shoulder, and a smile edged its way onto George's face as a reflex. It looked so uncomfortable on him.

"Yes, can I help you?" Sylvia said.

George turned around fast as if he expected to see someone he knew.

"Oh, I'm in no rush, I just wanted to buy this map. I can wait until you're done with him," the man said.

"It's alright. I can ring you up." Sylvia reached across George and forced him awkwardly aside as the man cautiously came forward.

As he placed the map down on the counter, George dropped the bones onto the ground, and Sylvia listened to them scatter like wood chips. George fell to his knees and picked them up frantically. His children all looked down together.

"Please, don't step back!" George yelled to the man.

The man bent down to help, but George batted him away. Sylvia leaned over, the counter pushing into her belly. George's jacket and shirt had ridden up his back, leaving a slice of pale skin exposed. She could see his white underwear bunching out over the waist of his pants as he stretched underneath a magazine rack to get at a piece, but the man quickly grabbed them off the floor before George could reach for them.

"Thank you," George said, breathing heavily.

"Don't mention it. What do you have there?" the man asked, pointing to George's fist.

"They're my wife's," George said, putting them back in his pocket.

"Guess everyone needs a hobby. Friend of mine does taxidermy on roadkill and sells them to places like these," he said, twirling his finger around. "Dresses them up funny with doll clothes. Some people like them. I saw you have one up front, how much is it?"

"I'm not sure," she said, thinking of her father stuffed and dressed in doll clothes.

George opened his jacket pocket and held it out as he carefully dropped the charred bones back in. The man looked at Sylvia like he was waiting for something more, but when she didn't say anything, the man held a hand up in goodbye and walked away. When the bell rang him out, Sylvia held her breath.

"I'm sorry. I haven't slept much," George said with his head down.

"It's fine."

"I should have told you who I am. I should have introduced myself," he said. "I'm George Sodder, what's your name?" he asked, sticking his hand out. He seemed to be breathing at a more even pace, now.

"Sylvia," she told him, again. She didn't want to touch him. Her palm was wet, but she couldn't wipe it off without him seeing. She put her hand in his and watched him to see if he'd react. He smiled.

"Sylvia?"

She nodded.

"My youngest daughter's name is Sylvia," he said.

"I'm sorry," she said.

He was confused for a moment and then his face softened.

"No, Sylvia's at home with my wife. She was sleeping with us that night when it happened."

"I see."

"My wife and I, we know they didn't die in that fire. They could be dead, but they didn't die in our house. We would have found something—anything of them, any part of them—but we didn't."

"Where did they go then?" Sylvia asked, nervously.

"Anywhere. I had enemies. People didn't like me—people don't like me. It could be ransom, you know, a kidnapping."

Sylvia hadn't eaten, and she needed to. Her stomach bubbled loud enough that George's eyes drifted down. She wanted to say she had to go to the bathroom, but she knew he would be here waiting for her when she came back.

"It's almost my lunch break," she said.

"I've been driving all night. Do you think I could get some coffee?"

"Sure, okay."

She didn't have the energy to make anything other than toast. She turned on the kettle and heated up the coffee left in there from the day before. She poured two cups and brought the toast out with jam and butter on a tray. He followed her to a booth and she sat down while wiping the dust and crumbs off onto her lap. It was hard for him to get in, his stomach pressing against the table that wouldn't give. She felt embarrassed for him, the way she would for her father when he tried to sit there, and stared out onto the highway instead of watching.

"Why did you call?" George asked again.

She wrapped her hands around her coffee mug.

"Ma'am?"

She could see him in the reflection of the window.

She could see how he struggled with every move he made, even the rise and fall of his shoulders as he breathed, even blinking. She didn't even let her use the phone.

"A family came in with children," Sylvia said.

She could see it differently, then. If she pretended, she could see it in a way that didn't make her own skin want to separate from her bones. The children wanted something sweet. They wanted pancakes and milk. That's what she liked as a child. Their fingers sticky with syrup strung between them. Her father would have been so mad.

"How many children?"

She took a bite of her toast and chewed slowly, then swallowed. He was patient; she wouldn't be able to wait him out.

"I don't remember. More than three, I think. It was a busy morning."

It wasn't busy, it's never busy here, they all said, speaking from the aisles in the store, from the heavy boxes, from underneath the tables.

"What did they look like?"

"Dark hair, but I don't know much else."

But you must remember our eyes, yes? Turn around. Look at us, then. See? They all said together, sounding like snakes.

"How did they seem?"

She turned and saw them there at the table behind her, but they weren't moving, just staring with dark eyes. She tried to see them eating, but they still had their mouths closed. Next to them, she saw her father—the way he was after the car hit him. Scraped beyond recognition and his chest bent backwards. His hands shook the cup of coffee he held.

"They seemed okay, sure. They seemed fine. If they were

your kids, and, like I said, I don't know, but if they were, they didn't seem like they were in trouble."

He sighed loudly, almost a sob, and his body seemed to deflate. Her shoulders dropped with his, and she exhaled. The tension in her arms had given. She no longer needed to consciously stop her body from quivering, and for a moment, she could look at his reflection in the glass without having to blur her vision out of shame. Then he started to shake his head.

But that's not how it went.

"That doesn't make any sense," he said.

"What's that?" She closed her eyes.

"If they seemed like they were alright, what was it that made you call? You would have had to remember something. I didn't place that ad for another month. Sylvia." He held her gaze in the glass. "What was it?"

She tried to cross one ankle over the other, but her foot hit the center pole, hard, making everything vibrate on the table.

"I wish I could help you more," she said.

George kept eyeing her reflection until the bell over the door rang, and a little girl ran in. She was about five or six years old and alone. Sylvia could see a man outside, leaning against the car. The girl, with braided, brown hair, looked around the store nervously until she saw them at the table.

"I need to use your bathroom!" she yelled.

Sylvia pointed to the door in the corner, and the little girl ran off. Without saying anything, George got up roughly, shaking the booth. He swung the door open violently, almost shaking the bell off. She watched him walk to his car, but he stopped at the man. She couldn't tell what he was saying, but he pointed at him aggressively, then back at her through the window, before stomping off. The man looked confused, and then his face became drawn. He started fast towards the door, not quite running, but urgent. He came in and shouted "Maria!" giving Sylvia a glance that cut through her middle. There was no answer. Sylvia's chest tightened and she pressed her back against the window.

"Maria!" He yelled again.

The girl came out scared, wiping her hands on her yellow eyelet dress, her big eyes wide and dark.

Mary Thorson lives and writes in Milwaukee, Wisconsin. She received her BA in Creative Writing from the University of Wisconsin-Milwaukee and her MFA from Pacific University in Oregon. Her stories have appeared in the Los Angeles Review, Reckon Review, Cotton Xenomorph, Milwaukee Noir, Worcester Review, Rock and a Hard Place, and Tough, among others. Her short story, "Book of Ruth," was included in *Best American Mystery & Suspense, '24*, edited by Steph Cha and S.A. Cosby. Her work has been nominated for Best American Short Stories, a Derringer, and a Pushcart Prize. She hangs out with her two feisty daughters, the best husband, and a dog named Pam when she isn't teaching high school English, reading, or writing ghost stories. She is represented by Lori Galvin at Aevitas Creative Management. She is currently working on a novel.

THE BUNKER

Roaa Eid

Every breath could be my last.

I already accepted that.

The cold of the wall behind my back and under my feet slowly spreads over every part of my body. I wonder what it will be like when it finally reaches my heart, and I can give up.

I can't remember when the war ended, if it ever did.

All I remember is the crash, the fire, the blood raining down like confetti on a never-ending parade.   I remember the rush into the bunker, so many people coming in—squeezing themselves end-to-end—to fit into its relative safety. I remember bodies disintegrating as easily as blowing a dandelion.

I remember death.

But in war, death is more like the prodigal son returning than an unwelcome companion. You run to it, embrace it, pray for its arrival. And now it is here.

In here, it's easy to forget the rest of the universe exists. The silence is absolute. Suffocating. Deafening.

I've never been afraid of the quiet before.

The food ran out sometime last week. I can't recall. There's no more water. And I am sure the air is getting thinner. Or I've just stopped being able to breathe it in very well. The lights are fading, I'm sure. Although, it has been getting harder to keep my eyes open. The pale greenish glow implies that the entire bunker is alight with illness. The whole place is sick. The whole place is *dying.*

I can smell it in the air. The whole place is heavy with the stench of the bodies spread out on the floor. The rot wafts in my nose, and I don't gag at it anymore. It pierces my skin, settles somehow into my bones, and yet I still do not balk at it.

It has become the smell of comfort. Of safety. Of home.

I am still. Silent. I haven't moved in days. Hours? Minutes?

I mirror the corpses around me.

Some smells here are hard to ignore sometimes, though. But I tell myself that the strong tang of urine and shit and vomit is nothing more than the smells of being human.

Do I remember what that's like?

We had to go in the one bunker that had been abandoned for several years, huh? No supplies, no radio, no survival.

I let my hand fall from my lap to my side. Or maybe it just falls on its own. It bumps into Sammy, who was sitting right next to me, and I automatically glance at him, knowing what I will see.

It takes my muddled brain too long to notice what isn't right.

His head is turned.

He is facing me.

I can see every line on his face, every pore, every hair on his chin.

He hadn't died like that. I made sure not to move anyone. I couldn't.

But now he had.

I wonder if I am finally losing my mind.

I lift my gaze and wander around the room.

Nothing changes. No surprises.

Everyone stays in their place. The dead are dead, and nothing moves beyond the slow opening and closing of my eyelids. The light rests on them, reflecting off the metal walls, and onto their skin, making it seem like they're glowing from within. All their eyes are closed. I made sure of that. After the first couple of times, when I would see the green glow of the fluorescents glittering back at me from the deep pits of their empty souls, I decided everyone would be better off sleeping anyway.

I tell myself to look at Sammy again, but this time I start at his feet. His boots are muddy and scuffed. There's dried blood on his pants leg from his injury coming into the bunker. His hands are clutching his torso, as though that might have filled it up with food. They're the color of chalk, a white so deep I'm sure he would have had no problem blending in with a pile of bleached bones.

He was one of the first to die, but his body still hasn't decided whether to rot or not. I force myself to go even further, to look at his face.

A scraggly red beard, filled with ash and blood.

Shriveled lips, a deep blue-black that made me think of whatever is found at the bottom of the ocean.

Snot running from a nose that was too big for his face, as always.

And wide, open eyes.

They look at me.

I look back.

They are as brown as they have always been. They are as glassy as the gaze of any corpse.

They blink.

For a second, I am motionless. For only one second, I am uncomprehending.

And for just that tiny, minuscule second, I am hopeful.

But then, I let my hand drift over to his neck, and I try to press my fingers against his pulse.

I find nothing.

His skin is as cold and dry as ever. It feels numb underneath my own. My fingers roam over his neck once more, trying to find life. It's like lowering my hand down into an infinite pit of ice, trying, hoping to find one shred of warmth.

He is unmoving, his eyes fixate on me, accusing me, as though I have failed for not finding life in him. I want to apologize to him, but with my lips crisscrossed with cracks, my throat like sandpaper, and not a single drop of moisture in my mouth, the words get lodged somewhere between my heart and the bunker.

And so there we sit. He doesn't blink again, and I try not to blink again, in case he blinks again. His chest does not move, and I try to still my own lungs. His pulse is nonexistent, and mine is running rampant through my body. The silence presses into my ears while the rush of my blood and the unsteady beat of my weakening heart are getting louder and louder by the moment.

Scrape.

After what felt like a lifetime in silence, the sound shakes me to my very core. My eyes swivel left and right, searching for the source. I look to the door, wondering if perhaps it will crack open now and I will see the sun, or the moon, or the sky, at least one more time.

That is when my eyes land on one of the foot soldiers that had made their way into the bunker with the rest.

Her leg is now bent at the knee.

And as I watch, another unbelievably loud scrape echoes throughout the room, as her other boot drags over the metal floor, so now both legs are bent. I look back at Sammy, and his face isn't turned to me any longer. He's also watching the soldier.

I can't move.

I'm mesmerized.

The soldier's arms bend unnaturally as she pushes herself to her feet. I hear her bones crack, her shifting clothes, every bump and bang on the floor. I miss the silence of the bunker.

I've never been afraid of noise before.

Every muscle in my body is wound tight, and I can feel the

shivering all the way into my bones. Before she —it— gets the chance to turn around and see me, I also force my legs under me and push myself off the wall. Without thinking, I look down, and freeze, captured by Sammy's gaze.

He's caught me.

He knows what I'm doing.

I'm leaving them.

Abandoning them.

He won't let me.

I run.

Or, at least, I try. My body is worn and weak. It has realized the fear, yet it is still too weary to act. My fingers dig into the wall, bleeding, bruised, and I dig into myself for some scrap of energy to push me forward.

The door is all the way on the other side, and there is a labyrinth of bodies between us that I am now too reluctant to touch. When they were standing, they were packed tightly, and now they're a tangle of limbs and blood that I am not willing to untangle. There are too few gaps between them on the floor for me to pass.

There is no path for the living through the dead.

I take one step towards the door.

The soldier turns around.

I refuse to look at her, to look into her eyes.

I refuse to look at any of them as I find the floor in the crook of someone's elbow, in the gap between their legs, in the space between one's hand and another's neck. My feet barely skim the ground before I'm gone.

More sounds fill the space that the silence used to torment. More scrapes and something tells me Sammy is coming after me.

Sammy isn't going to let me go. Not now. Not ever.

From the corner of my eyes, legs twitch, and clothes ruffle, and one by one, as the door grows closer, they stand.

The dead rise.

My body is cold. It's almost like the metal walls never left it, and it's growing numb and frozen by the second. With every step closer to the door, the more my bones weigh heavier and sink; the more my heart beats slower and slower, and the blood rushing through my body becomes sluggish; the more my vision blurs, and the palish green light seems to fade deeper into black.

But I'm almost there, almost there, almost there…

A gasp.

I hear it, and it takes a while to understand that it came from me. It takes an even longer time to identify the problem.

A hand is wrapped around my ankle.

The boy is facedown, and his jacket is shredded so badly that it's barely there. I can see the shrapnel embedded into the skin of his back. The blood is dry, the skin flaking, and I can see just how deep every piece dug into the flesh. I can almost hear the explosion that had killed him, smell the gunpowder, taste the metal shavings and the blood in my mouth. He had been dead before the bunker door closed.

If there was any water left inside me, tears would spring to my eyes. A scream born deep from my chest builds upwards, until nothing is holding it back but my lips pressed firmly together. I tug my foot, hoping to pull it out of his grip. But it is like iron. And my strength is slowly fading.

For one moment, I consider just leaving my foot behind. To continue for the door, and let my leg just rip out of its socket. He can keep it. But the second I turn away from him and try to take one step, I fall.

I never thought life could be in slow motion. But as I see the floor rise to meet me, it feels like time is slowing down in our little bunker. Yet, there is no time for me to turn away from the body laid out in front of me. My hands extended before me, hoping to catch myself, do nothing as I crash onto someone's torso. I know it's impossible, but I think my hands break through his ribs and somehow meet his silent heart.

I look up, one last glance at the door, my hand extended, my fingers reaching, reaching, and skimming its surface before I'm dragged backward. I try to claw at the floor, but my hands either meet metal that is too smooth or bodies that are too dead. There is more than one hand on my legs now. I let the scream go free, and it tears through my throat like a dying animal begging for mercy. The only other sounds are the shuffling of boots on the floor, and my body as it's dragged across the bunker. Their grip tightens as I try to kick them off, and the bones in my legs groan. I keep pulling and tugging until I hear a snap, and my scream turns into a howl of pain. They don't stop, unbothered by anything other than the immediate task at hand.

The dead do not make a sound.

In the end, I'm back to my place at the wall, and my screams turn to whimpers and then silence. My body goes limp as every shred of energy I had mustered falls out. Rough hands grab my shoulders and push my back to the wall so that I am sitting where I'd been. Then, one by one, the dead walk back to their places and fall to the floor. The foot soldier looks back only once at me, but I don't return her gaze.

Sammy is by my side. He lies back down, and just before closing his eyes, he extends his hand and grabs onto mine.

And the dead, with me sleeping among them, rest again.

Roaa Eid is a writer, poet, and researcher based in Egypt, with a BA in English Literature and an MA in Medieval Studies. She started writing when she was twelve years old and realized words and fiction made great friends during lonely teenage years. You can find her work in Brief Encounters, Saffron City Press, Aloka Magazine, and The Brussels Review. One of her poems will also be an Honorable Mention in the 2024 Art of Unity Literary Award. She likes to explore the real, the impossible, the emotional — ultimately, what makes humans question everything.

Ahuizotl

Victor De Anda

You're just another asshole, but she doesn't know that yet. Nobody does.

We're sitting at the bar when Carol flips the blonde curls away from her angular cheekbones. Is she bored? At school she's prim and proper, but tonight she looks drop-dead dangerous. Her face glows in the light of the Kentucky Club, her perfume a mix of sweet and earthy scents.

Say something. Don't let this date die before it's even started.

Something catches Carol's eye and gives me the chance to steal a look at the rest of her. The geometric shapes on her tight-fitting sweater dress contrast with the winding curves of her body. My eyes blink hard to make sure all of this is real. It is, and she's the diamond in this shitty Juarez dive bar, that's for sure.

The bar's front door crashes open and another clump of noisy Americans pours inside—a menagerie of jocks, nerds, and sorority girls. It's just another Saturday night in J-Town. All kinds flock to Juarez from across the border in El Paso and points beyond. Not for the sights, but for the drinking. No matter who you are, your American money's good here. As long as you're seventeen or look like it, no one cares.

Compliment her.

My eyes meet Carol's again. "You smell really nice," I say. "What's that perfume you're wearing?"

She cracks a smile, her cheeks flush. "You're sweet, Richie," she says. "It's called Giorgio."

"Giorgio, huh? I'll have to make a note of that," I say.

She looks at something else off to the side. "Can you believe that we're seniors?" she says. "You apply to any colleges yet?"

Keep the conversation going. Tell her something personal.

I try to draw her attention back. "I want to go to film school, maybe USC or UCLA, but my parents think I should stick to journalism. How about you?"

She looks at me again. "I haven't decided on a major, so I'll probably just do general ed classes at UTEP."

Just then, a trio of young Republicans in button-downs and boat shoes wedge themselves between the two of us, vying for the bartender's attention. They all look fresh-faced and ready to vote for Reagan again. One of them runs his eyes all over Carol. He's wearing a Phi Tau pledge pin.

"Carol Perkins?" he says.

She looks up at him from her barstool. "Jerry? Hey, what are you doing here?"

His face lights up like he's been handed an oversized check from the Publisher's Clearing House sweepstakes. "Just out with the guys. You want some company?"

Carol glances over at me. "I'm here with my friend Richie Alvarez. Do you know him?"

Friend.

The frat dude spins around to face me and offers his hand. "Hey man, I'm Jerry, nice to meet you."

What an asshole.

I smile without showing my teeth. "What's up."

Jerry pulls his hand back and yanks a twenty from his jeans pocket. He holds it up to grab the bartender's attention. In his other hand is a slip of neon pink paper. "Oh, check this out," he says, passing the flyer to Carol. "There's a freak show at one of the bars around here. Some place called Nosferatu."

Carol glances at the flyer then hands it to me. "Sounds creepy."

The bartender appears. "Si señores, what would you like to drink?"

"Tres cervezas, por favor," Jerry says. He glances at Carol. "You want another one?"

She smiles. "Sure, thanks."

Jerry doesn't ask me. Instead, he addresses the bartender. "Make that four Coronas, gracias."

The bartender walks away when Jerry turns to me. "Sorry dude, did you want another beer?"

"No thanks," I say. "I'm good."

Jackass.

Jerry's buddies drop back to check out the club's surroundings. I study the flyer to find out more about the freak show. Jerry drones on to Carol about what it's like to pledge a fraternity.

I interrupt the conversation. "Carol, we should go check out this Ahuizotl."

"Ahh wee what?" Carol says.

Jerry frowns.

"AHH-WEE-ZOH-TULL," I sound it out for them. "The great Aztec water dog. It could be fun. Make our date more interesting."

Jerry's eyebrows slide up his face. "Oh shit," he says. "You two are here on a date? I didn't realize—"

The bartender shows up with the beers. Jerry hands them to Carol and his buddies.

Carol's face turns stiff. "I wouldn't call it a date—" she says.

Be strong.

"It was going great until you showed up," I tell Jerry.

Jerry steps back, his hands raised in surrender. "Say no more dude, I'll leave you two alone now. Carol, let's catch up soon." Jerry and his buddies head off to the dance floor just beyond the bar.

Carol doesn't say anything.

Now play it cool.

I drum my hands on the bar top. "So how do you know Jerry?"

"He graduated from Northwood last year, don't you remember him?"

I spin on my barstool to face Carol. "Nope, can't say that I do."

Carol looks surprised. "He took the varsity basketball team to the state finals last year? He got a full scholarship to UTEP."

"Never went to a game," I say. "Sports just aren't my thing."

Carol shakes her head in disapproval. "They're not for everyone, I guess."

As if on cue, the Kentucky Club's jukebox comes to life with the wavering synthesizer sounds of Prince's "Let's Go Crazy."

"Oh my God, I love this song," Carol says. "Have you heard it yet?" She lip-syncs the opening sermon.

Her face glows and my heart thrums like I'm on the first drop of a rollercoaster.

The song kicks into high gear when Prince screams, and groups of kids scramble to the dance floor.

"You wanna dance?" she yells into my ear.

Fuck. Anything but dancing.

I grimace and lean into her ear. "Maybe, I've got to go to the men's room."

"What?" she says over the music.

"I need to pee."

Carol gives me a half-hearted smile. "Oh, okay," she says.

"I'll be right back," I tell her.

She gives me the thumbs up and takes another swig of her beer.

‡

In the men's room I stand at the aluminum trough and piss into it. The trough is filled with ice, which is weird.

Why did she have to ask me to dance?

I avoid tipping the men's room attendant and head back out to our spot at the bar. But Carol's stool is empty. The Prince song is still blaring, the dance floor is crowded with gyrating kids, but there's no sign of her. My eyes search the club. Jerry's buddies are still standing on the sidelines, checking out the drunk girls dancing with each other. Jerry's not with them. Him and Carol are both gone.

What the fuck.

‡

The crisp October air slaps me in the face as I step outside the club. The street's crowded with more American high school and college kids, all of them carousing like it's spring break. Lots of yelling and drunken conversations. The restaurants and clubs lining the main drag light up the night with their neon signs and flashing bulbs.

On the horizon, the distant lights of El Paso shimmer through a curtain of Mexican haze. I check my watch. 10pm. I've got a midnight curfew, but I'm willing to miss it for the chance to kiss Carol.

She bailed on you. Leave her ass here and go home.

I push through the crowds, passing various food vendors on

the sidewalk with their portable grills. The air's thick with the savory smells of carne asada and pork for street tacos. I should feel hungry, but instead it's nausea that's creeping through me.

I make my way down the row of clubs and restaurants. Short, stocky men stand in front of each doorway, calling out to the passing crowd like carnival barkers. "Drink especiales tonight!" "Ladies get in free!" "Chicas Bonitas!"

A local walks past me and hands me a flyer as he shouts. "Come see the eighth wonder of the world! Ahuiztol, the great Water Dog and protector! Only at Nosferatu! No cover for the ladies!" I pocket the flyer.

Further down the block at the next traffic light, the crowds have thinned out. It's mostly just locals walking around this part of town. A panaderia stands at the corner, its lights still on at this hour. The front door opens and the sugary smells of cookies and cakes floats out into the street. Maybe I should get some pan dulce for Carol. Or does she even like Mexican sweet bread?

A girl's laughter fills the air. It sounds like Carol. I step inside the panaderia to investigate. No sign of her. When I come back out, I hear the laughter again. It's close. I peek around the corner and my chest snaps like a rubber band that's been wrapped too tight.

No fucking way.

Carol leans up against the side of the panaderia while Jerry towers over her, his left hand caressing her curly hair. He turns away to take a drag off a cigarette, then hands it to her. Carol holds the cigarette in her long fingers and pulls Jerry's face closer to hers. They kiss long and hard.

My eyelids flutter, and I step back behind the corner. My heart pounds so loud that my ears ache from the pulsing.

Enough of this bullshit, just go home.

Instead I take a deep breath and head towards them, my

muscles tightening. Jerry notices me and backs away from Carol, straightening his posture. He's Frankenstein-tall and nothing but arms and legs.

"There you are," I say to Carol. "Was wondering where you went."

Jerry takes a long hit off his cigarette and stares me down. He even gives me a slight smile.

"We just stepped out for a smoke." Carol brushes the hair away from her face and looks at me. " We were about to head back, weren't we, Jerry?"

"Yeah, sure," Jerry says.

My eyes dart back and forth between the two of them.

She's here with you. Show her who's boss.

My tongue's paralyzed.

Carol looks at me with defiant eyes. "You got something to say, Richie?"

I shake my head and stare at the ground. "Y-You had me worried for a minute, that's all."

Pathetic.

"I can take care of myself, Richie," Carol says. "Thank you, though."

Jerry walks past me and gives me a tap on the shoulder. "No need to worry, dude."

Jackass.

I reach into my back pocket and pull out the Nosferatu flyer. I hand it to Carol. "Why don't we check out this Ahuizotl thing? Sounds like fun, right?"

Jerry stops and turns around. "Now that's the best idea I've heard all night."

Carol studies the flyer and nods. "I don't know, I'm not good with scary stuff."

I try standing as tall as I can, hoping Carol notices. She doesn't. "Don't worry, I'll make sure you're okay."

Jerry laughs and shoves me from behind. "C'mon, Carol, it'll be fun. I'll see if the guys want to go too."

Tell this motherfucker to piss off.

I spin around to face Jerry. "I was talking to Carol." My voice cracks. "No one's inviting you."

Jerry laughs and stubs out his cigarette on the sidewalk. He glances at Carol, then gives me a fierce stare. "Do you mind if we tag along, Carol?"

Carol nods her head and shrugs. "Nope," she says. Then she looks at me. "C'mon Richie. The more the merrier?"

"Fine," I say. "Let's all go, then."

"Alright, it's settled," Jerry says. "Don't worry Richie, we'll make sure this water dog doesn't get you."

Punch this dickhead.

☦

It's 10:30 by the time we get to Nosferatu. Located just a few blocks off the main drag, the bar has seen better days. The sign above the door is rusted, with multiple burned-out light bulbs on it. A steady crowd of American kids pulses in and out of the club, so it can't be too dangerous. The freak show's probably just a marketing ploy to drum up business.

Inside, the bar's long and narrow, its walls painted crimson red. The air's heavy with clove cigarette smoke. Round tables fill the space. No dance floor here. The vibe's more sinister than the Kentucky Club. The lighting's dimmer too, the corners of the club are dark and shadowy. I squint to see several entangled couples sitting at the tables, using the darkness as cover for their behavior.

More of a make-out place I guess. "True" by Spandau Ballet plays, but I can't tell where the jukebox is.

"Cool place," Jerry says. "The guys are missing out."

"Too bad they didn't want to come," I say. "We could use more meat at this sausage fest."

Carol chuckles. It's the first time I've made her laugh tonight.

Jerry looks at both me and Carol. "My sausage is all you need."

Carol steals a glance at Jerry.

A bartender walks to the end of the counter and puts a microphone to his mouth. The metallic screech of audio feedback fills the air for a second before he speaks over the bar's PA system.

"Damas y caballeros…ladies and gentlemen…please head to the green door at the back of the bar to see the one, the only AHUIZOTL! Tickets for the show are just cinco dolares, only five dollars! Apologies, but the show price is separate from the cover charge. Bring your drinks if you like."

Carol pulls a crumpled twenty-dollar bill from her purse. "This one's on me," she says. "I owe you both for the beers and for driving, Richie."

"No worries, but thank you," I say.

Jerry laughs. "It's about time you paid for something."

We line up at the green door, along with a group of other willing American students. The bartender walks up and opens the door. Beyond it, a long, dark hallway stretches back, a single faint light burning at the end of it. The bartender turns to us with an open palm. "How many?"

Carol hands him the money. "Three, please."

The bartender gives her a big smile and rips the tickets from his roll, handing them to each of us. Then he gives Carol her change and motions for us to enter the hallway. "Muchas gracias, please hand your tickets to the man at the end of the hallway. Enjoy the show, and remember, no touching or feeding Ahuizotl. Buenas noches."

Our group steps into the hallway as the bartender shuts the door behind us. The light is dim. The air reeks of shit, piss, and wet straw.

"My god," Carol says, covering her mouth and nose with her hand.

The hallway pulses with an eerie orange glow from the single light source at the end of the hallway. A man's voice emanates from it. "Bienvenidos, welcome ladies and gentlemen. Please walk towards the light. Ahuizotl will arrive shortly," he says.

Carol and Jerry shuffle ahead of me down the narrow hallway. The other people in the group scoot along behind me.

As we move forward, Carol and Jerry walk side by side.

My eyes are getting accustomed to the dark when I notice Jerry's hand grazing Carol's backside.

What the hell?

Jerry's palming Carol's ass cheek like a basketball and her hand's on top of his, guiding it, massaging it. My pulse quickens and my head swirls.

Fuck this shit. Leave both of their asses now. Just go.

Something grows in the pit of my stomach. It's the same dread that builds when the teacher chooses me to read out loud in Social Studies. Or when the assholes in Phys Ed play keep-away with my underwear in the locker room after class. But instead of running away from the feeling like I usually do, this time I embrace it.

When we reach the light at the end of the hallway, there's another room off to the left. Camping lanterns hang on the walls inside. Several people in our group hack and cough from the stench, which is even stronger back here. Straight ahead of us at the end of the hallway is another door with a backlit red EXIT sign above it.

A man appears from inside the low-lit room. He's built like a fireplug. He grabs our tickets and stretches out his arm with a welcoming gesture. "Please come in, ladies and gentlemen, but stay against the left wall. Ahuizotl will be here soon." He walks out the back exit door.

Our group creeps inside the room and hugs the left wall. A makeshift holding pen made of chicken wire and two-by-fours stands alongside the opposite wall. Hay covers the floor beyond the pen.

"This is so weird," says one of the other kids in our party.

"I smell a rip-off," Jerry says.

The back exit door creaks open and everyone turns toward the sound. Heavy footsteps and the pitter-patter of tiny-clawed feet fill the air. The back door closes with a thud.

The fireplug guy reappears and cups his hands around his mouth like a megaphone. "Please step back, ladies and gentlemen, and say hello to Ahuizotl, the Aztec wonder of the world! He is glad to see you."

The little footsteps get closer, along with what sounds like a chain. Ahuizotl and his handler enter the dim light of the room.

Our group lets out a collective gasp. One of the girls behind us lets out a drunk guffaw instead.

Ahuizotl is the size of a small dog with pointed ears and dark, wet fur. He gets led behind the chicken wire pen and stares at us with colorless eyes.

"What the fuck?" Jerry says, pointing at the creature.

The handler unclips the chain link leash so that Ahuizotl can move around freely behind the chicken wire barrier.

Two drunk girls behind me push their way out. "Fuck this, we're getting the hell out of here," one of them says. The fireplug guy escorts them to the back exit door.

"Thank you ladies, buenas noches," he says as they leave.

Ahuizotl paces along the chicken wire barrier, eyeing us intently.

The handler speaks up. "Do not be afraid of Ahuizotl, unless of course, you have polluted our country's waters."

"What the fuck is it?" Jerry asked.

The handler doesn't acknowledge Jerry. "Ahuizotl, translated from the Aztec language, means 'water dog.' The ahuizotl were sent by the gods to protect the rivers and lakes of Mexico. This one protects the Rio Grande right here in Juarez. Take a closer look, if you like."

The creature stops and stands on its hind legs, its fleshy tail writhing. It grabs onto the chicken wire barrier with its tiny fingers. Ahuizotl lets out a piercing wail like a cranky baby.

The handler pulls out a red tomato from a paper bag and holds it up for everyone to see. "Ahuizotl is hungry, that is why he cries. In ancient times, he would feast on human eyes, nails, and teeth. Nowadays, he enjoys tomatoes. Perhaps it reminds him of what his ancestors ate long ago."

Carol puts a hand to her mouth. "This is fucking crazy," she says. Jerry puts his arm around her and she wraps hers around him. She slides her hand into the back pocket of his Levi's. My chest hurts again from all this touchy-feely stuff.

Why not me?

The creature cries again and stares at us with his pleading eyes. His fur is spiky from being wet, his skin-colored tail long and muscular. Ahuizotl's got to be a possum, it's the only explanation.

My eyes are drawn back to Carol and Jerry. Now Jerry's hand has lifted up her sweater dress from behind. I see a flash of Carol's bare butt cheek as Jerry caresses it.

Carol lets out a faint gasp. "Stop it, Jerry." She shoves his hand away to cover herself again.

I can barely hear anything now over the lub-dub filling my ears. My heart pounds like a jackhammer in overdrive.

Ahuizotl spots the tomato and becomes agitated. He rubs his tiny hands together, eager for a taste. The handler reaches down behind the chicken wire barrier and hands Ahuizotl the vegetable. Ahuizotl grabs it and begins gnawing into it eagerly. His teeth are small and sharp.

"Oh my god," Carol says. "Look at him eat."

Jerry pulls away from Carol to get closer to Ahuizotl. "This is a joke," he says. "It's just a possum."

The handler puts himself between Jerry and Ahuizotl. "Señor, please step back. Do not startle Ahuizotl. He is very excitable. Please."

Jerry gets into the handler's face. "We want our money back."

Carol hops up to Jerry and tugs on the belt loops of his jeans. "C'mon baby, don't freak him out."

My head throbs and my stomach's doing somersaults.

What the fuck is going on?

"Jerry, let's just get out of here," Carol pleads. "We should be heading home anyways."

Jerry pushes her off and addresses the handler. "We're not leaving until we get our money back," he slurs. "You understand refundo, señor?"

I creep up to the chicken-wire barrier and Ahuizotl moves toward me, looking for more food.

The handler shakes his head and raises his hands. "I do not carry any money, señor. You will need to talk to the bartender. I'm sorry you are not enjoying the show."

Carol yanks the back of Jerry's shirt. "Let's just go. You can stay in my room tonight."

Jerry glares at Carol. "I'm getting your money back first." Then he gets into the handler's face even more. "You owe us fifteen dollars, amigo. Quince dolares, comprende?"

The handler isn't backing down. He's probably seen his share of drunk Americans before.

White flashes stab my eyes and my head swirls. Tonight's been a shitstorm from the start.

I look into Ahuizotl's hungry black eyes as I lean in even closer to the barrier. He's panting hard now, saliva dripping from his small, sharp teeth. I reach into my front pants pocket and search for an offering. I unwrap it and present it to Ahuizotl. He almost smiles at me when he sees it. Then he snatches the Tootsie Roll from my palm and gnaws on it like a five-year-old satisfying their sugar tooth.

Ahuizotl's handler notices what I'm doing. He turns away from Jerry toward me. "Señor, please, don't feed the animal," he says. "He will only want more."

Jerry seizes the moment to give the handler a kidney punch from behind. The handler recoils from the hit.

"We want our fucking money," Jerry says as he jabs at the handler again. Now the handler's fed up, he spins around and throws a left hook that catches Jerry in the ribs.

The rest of the kids in our group run out of the room and out the back exit door.

Carol tries to hold Jerry back, grasping for a handhold.

"Leave me alone," Jerry says, shoving her off. "I'm getting

your money back."

Ahuizotl swallows the last half of the Tootsie Roll without chewing and licks his lips. He climbs to the top of the chicken-wire barrier to get closer to me and more food. All the commotion is making Ahuizotl even more agitated as he lets out a deep growl.

"Jerry, let's go NOW," Carol screams. She gets behind Jerry to pull him away when he cocks his right arm back for another swing. The sound of crunching celery fills the air as his elbow connects with her nose. Carol cries out and puts her hands to her face, blood dripping down the front of her sweater.

Carol stares in shock at her hands, wet with crimson. "You're a real asshole, Jerry!"

Jerry turns and reaches out to Carol. "Sorry babe, I didn't see you there."

The handler sees an opening and pummels Jerry in the ear. All this does is piss off Jerry even more. He throws another punch back at the handler.

I glare at Jerry and Carol and back at Ahuizotl. All of this is Jerry's fault. He's fucked up everything tonight. I reach down into the pen and grab Ahuizotl by the tail with my bare hand. He grips the fence with his tiny fingers and hisses at me.

After a few seconds of me tugging on his tail, Ahuizotl relents and lets go of the chicken-wire. His body writhes in the air as I hold him up like a prize. I offer him up to Jerry and the handler.

The handler sees what I've done. "No señor, please don't!" he shouts.

Jerry turns to me and I fling Ahuizotl at him. The creature lands on Jerry's chest and claws away at it, shredding Jerry's shirt until he gets to exposed skin. Ahuizotl lets out a high-pitched wail like a siren.

Jerry stumbles backwards, grabbing at Ahuizotl. "Get this

fucking thing off me!"

The handler wipes the blood from his mouth and reaches into his back pocket for some heavy-duty gloves. He puts them on and reaches out for the animal. "Señor, take it easy, let me get him for you."

Jerry's not listening. Instead he's trying to grab Ahuizotl's whipping tail, but he can't get a hold of it. Ahuizotl sinks his teeth into Jerry's chest and bites off a chunk of flesh. Jerry lets out a scream. Ahuizotl tears off another mouthful.

I turn to see how Carol's doing. She's holding a wad of bloody tissues to her nose.

"I got you now, you little fucker," Jerry yells. He manages to get a grip on Ahuizotl's tail and yanks him off his chest. Blood stains cover Jerry's shirt as he holds Ahuizotl out at arm's length.

"Señor, please," the handler says. "Give him to me."

Ahuizotl snarls as Jerry holds him in the air by his tail like a fish he's caught at the lake.

"I'll give this little fucker back, alright," Jerry says.

Jerry spins Ahuizotl by his tail like a hammer thrower.

"Jerry, no," Carol shouts. Her nose is swollen now, her mouth and chin covered in dried blood.

Ahuizotl is a blur as Jerry spins him hard. Then he lets go of the animal and everything moves in slow motion. Ahuizotl sails through the air towards the back wall. The handler reaches out for his beloved creature but is too late, his mouth wide open in a scream. Ahuizotl is oblivious to the impending impact.

Back in real time, Ahuizotl hits the back wall with a dull, wet thud. Blood splatters on the dingy wallpaper as his body bounces and then drops to the floor. Ahuizotl is either stunned or badly injured.

The handler places his gloved hands on Ahuizotl's motionless body and turns to Jerry. "Señor, I suggest you leave before I call the police."

I walk over to Carol and put my hand on her shoulder. "Let me take you home," I say.

"Fuck off, Richie," she says. "Coming here was your idea. This is all your fault."

I glance over at Jerry. He catches his breath and looks around the room. He looks back at Carol. "We need to get the fuck out of here," he says.

He's right.

I make my way out the exit door without looking back once. Behind me, I hear Carol and Jerry whispering apologies to one another and trading consoling kisses. My heart feels like a brick in my chest.

Outside, the crisp October air cools my face and clears the shit stink from my nose. A police siren blares in the distance, moving closer. I check my watch. 1:20 am. Beyond the alley, along the far horizon, I can make out the lights of El Paso across the border. Time to go home and get a talking-to from my worried parents. I'll probably get grounded, but I don't care.

Carol will tell all her friends about tonight. By the end of school on Monday, everyone will know what an asshole I am. That might not be a bad thing after all.

Victor De Anda is a writer in Philadelphia who enjoys watching movies and searching for good Mexican food. His fiction has been published in *Dark Waters Vol. 1*, Guilty Crime Story Magazine, Mystery Tribune, Shotgun Honey, The Yard: Crime Blog, and Punk Noir, with more forthcoming. He is on BlueSky @victordeanda.bsky.social and you can find out more at https://linktr.ee/victordeanda

Mad Mara

Joel Nedecky

I asked Jay Hanrahan into the room, provided earplugs, and explained how the MRI machine would record images of his hip. Hanrahan struggled to lay down, and when he'd finally achieved that feat, I pressed the button, sliding him into the cylinder.

■ ■ ■

Most people don't realize how loud an MRI machine gets, with a loud whir, the occasional rattle, and a low, continuous hum. The futuristic-looking device was reminiscent of a mini spaceship.

Last week I'd dyed my hair and cut three inches off. I wore oversized dark-rimmed glasses. I kept the lighting in the room low. In nurse's scrubs, I felt like a different person. He wouldn't recognize me.

"You'll be inside for thirty minutes," I said. "Please try to remain still."

"Thirty minutes?" he gasped. "Jesus…that long?"

I smiled. "Yes."

I'd been waiting for this moment for two years. In fact, I'd been standing next to my son's grave the first time I thought about killing Jay Hanrahan. After the accident, several people told me "Living well would be the best revenge," but they had never lost a child to a drunk driver.

The best revenge is not living well. The best revenge is *revenge.*

I stayed in bed for weeks after Cody passed. My husband, Logan, begged me to get up. "At least try," he said. "You're strong. You can do it. At least try to move forward."

Move forward?

I told Logan I was done trying, and I would never smile and move forward, knowing what happened to Cody was possible. That it could happen to someone else.

Logan left soon after, which seemed to be a turning point, and one afternoon, a seismic shift occurred. Or maybe it had been coming on slowly and I just never felt it.

You can kill him.

A whisper in the shadows at first, but soon the words grew louder.

You can kill him.

Then they were a roar.

You can kill him.

I got out of bed, made coffee, and ate two pieces of toast. On a whim, I drove to the Y, purchased a membership, and lifted weights. After, I showered and bought groceries. I combed my hair and put on makeup. I brushed my teeth.

The next day I did it again.

And again.

And again.

Ten-minute workouts grew to twenty, then thirty, and soon an hour. Sometimes more. Having quit my job, I had the time. I started learning about calories, protein, carbs, and fats. I ate well. I read. I enrolled in a jiu-jitsu class. I watched movies.

And a year later, in the best physical shape of my life, I went to court each day to watch the trial and almost died a second time when Harahan's lawyer got the results of his blood sample tossed out. Hospital officials made an error while collecting the sample immediately following his arrest. As a result, Hanrahan was found guilty of dangerous driving but not manslaughter. He was sentenced to time served, a year.

One. Fucking. Year.

For killing my son.

I listened to the judge deliver the sentence, contemplating how I'd kill Jay Hanrahan, the voice so loud I looked over my shoulder to make sure no one else could hear it.

You can kill him.

I could shoot Hanrahan, but that didn't seem like enough. He drove over my son like he was a speed bump.

I could stab Hanrahan, but he was big, twice my size, and I'd have to sneak up on him and slit his throat. Much too messy.

I could hit him with my car. There was a certain poetry to it that I liked, but there were several ways a body could deflect that meant death could not be guaranteed.

None of those options did justice to the crime perpetrated against my boy. Then one night, as I re-read transcripts of the trial, I read the line that changed everything. I'd missed it watching in person, but reading it later, the ink on the page flickered neon, bright, clear, and true, like the sign above a nightclub.

Hanrahan was on the stand, and in response to a question he made an off-the-cuff remark: "I got a bad hip."

I hired a private investigator, who somehow accessed Hanrahan's medical records. Hanrahan saw a doctor a month before he'd killed my son. An x-ray showed he had osteoarthritis, a degenerative condition for which there was no cure. At some point, he'd need an MRI to confirm the damage, and eventually, a new hip. When he was arrested and awaiting trial, the process got put on hold. As a free man, Hanrahan visited a doctor and the process started anew.

There was a six-to-ten month wait for an MRI, so I bribed a woman to schedule Hanrahan's appointment at the high end of that window and enrolled in the eight-month MRI Technician and Spectroscopy program the next day.

We learned about pathology, applications, procedures, instrumentation, sectional anatomy, and patient care. The last sixteen weeks were a practicum, where a veteran technician observed and guided the student experience. I was thirty-five and the oldest person in my class, but I became comfortable as the 'old woman,' as my classmates affectionately said, and the work was fine, albeit not overly fulfilling.

Finally, I took the Canadian Association of Medical Radiation Technologists certification exam, passed with flying colors, and accepted a position at the St. Boniface Clinic.

☦

Hanrahan became noticeably agitated thirty-two minutes into the MRI. "Hey…how much time is left?"

I spoke into the microphone wired into speakers inside the machine. "Cody. Rust."

Hanrahan froze, then his body jerked as if electrocuted, and he banged his head. "Fuck!"

I watched him squirm on the monitor, as I let my son's name sink in.

"How'd you know about that?" he cried. "I served my time… I paid my debt to society!"

There was scorn in his voice, like he'd been the one who'd suffered. He continued to thrash, trying to snake his way out of the machine, but the tray was locked. . Perhaps a smaller, nimble person could have gotten out, but not one as big as Hanrahan.

"Let me out!" he screamed. "What is this? Let me out!"

I sunk the needle into the soft crevice between his first and second toes, released the drugs, and closed my eyes. I waited to make sure he was unconscious, then activated the power and slid the rack out. I moved the stretcher next to the rack, taking my time, remembering all those heavy weights I'd lifted in preparation for this moment.

Hanrahan weighed two-seventy-five. I'd never deadlifted that amount—my one rep max was one-seventy—but he was elevated, so it was less about lifting and more about controlling his bulk. If I went too fast, Hanrahan's momentum would cause him to roll off the stretcher onto the floor and I'd never get him up, not without help.

I stood behind the stretcher, bent at the knees, and pulled, slowly rolling him, inch by inch, pound by pound until he tipped, falling face first onto the stretcher.

I covered him with a blanket, wheeled him out the back door, and repeated the roll, sending Hanrahan into the back of my Kia Sorento, his left arm and leg protruding like unruly strands of hair poking out of a ball cap. I folded him in, closed the hatch, and went back inside to tidy up.

‡

The first thing I did was starve him. A sip of water every five hours. No food the first two days. On day three I went into the room.

"My name's Mara Rust," I said. "Do you know who I am?"

Hanrahan lunged, causing the restraints to pull taut. "Fuck you!"

"You're going to talk to me about my son. His name was Cody."

Hanrahan's eyes flared at the name with recognition. He flung his weight side to side, but it was no use. He was restrained in a GhostBed Flex Adjustable. It had cost me four grand, but it was worth it. I could bring him into the upright position without removing the cuffs, and the structural integrity of the unit was such that he couldn't break the frame.

"Tell me about that day," I said.

Hanrahan just shook his head.

I took to eating supper in the room. Butter chicken with white rice. Pulled pork on a bun. The smelliest meals I could think of, and I made orgasmic noises as I ate.

On day four, I beat him with a bar of soap I'd tucked inside a sock. Then I dragged a piece of paper across his arms and legs. Death by a thousand cuts.

"Tell me about that day," I said again.

"Fuck you, you crazy bitch!"

It was Sunday—day five—when the conversation happened. I fed Hanrahan a piece of dry bread and water, and sat down with a plate of nachos covered in ground beef, cheese, and salsa. I took a bite, moaned euphorically, and waited.

"This isn't going to change anything…" he said. "You kidnapping me. The torture…"

I chewed, then took a sip of water. "You're probably right."

"So then why do it? Your kid's dead—"

I stood suddenly and stepped toward him, but not of my own volition. My body had reacted without my brain telling it what to do. He threw his hands up to protect himself. Fists cocked, I froze.

Breathe.

I let my arms fall and sat again, my chest in my throat.

"Do you remember the accident?" I said.

Hanrahan sent a look my way and sighed. "No. I don't remember a Goddamn thing. I was… I'd been drinking."

"In court, during the trial, one of the things I couldn't wrap my head around is how you didn't seem remorseful."

"How would you know that? How would you know how I felt?"

"Because I watched you. I saw the smile on your face at sentencing. You looked like you'd won."

"I don't know what to say to that," he said, but some of the intensity had melted away. "You want me to say I wasn't happy to get a short sentence and I can't do that. But I didn't think I'd won, I thought… I don't know what I thought."

He paused and I wondered if bringing him here was going to bring me the closure I craved so much.

"What were you hoping for?" he asked, interrupting my

thoughts.

"The death penalty…"

"There is no death penalty in Canada."

"There should be." I leaned forward, then sat back. "I wanted a life sentence: twenty-five years."

"I was drunk…"

"That's no excuse, you fucking asshole! That's…" I faded out, tired and feeling stuck, like I was floundering in quicksand. "You know, I had a speech ready to go. I even wrote it out." I pulled the paper from the pocket of my jeans. "Now, I don't know what to say to you."

"A speech…" Hanrahan grunted out a laugh. "You people…"

"What does that mean? Who's 'you people?'"

"You—rich people."

"I'm not rich," I said, jolted upright by his claim. "I have a regular job. My ex had a regular job. We're… normal."

"Really?" He tilted his head back and eyeballed the room dramatically. "Luxury vinyl plank flooring. Built-in shelves. Six-inch baseboards and crown molding." He planted his gaze on me. "If the rest of the house is like this, it must be worth three-quarters of a mill. What kind of car you drive?"

I hesitated.

"BMW? Mercedes?" He smirked. "Oh, no, wait—it's a Range Rover, isn't it?"

I didn't need to answer, but for some reason I did.

"BMW coupe," I said.

"And what does your husband do?"

"My ex-husband," I corrected. "He works in finance."

"Finance…" he scoffed. "Lady, you're rich."

I'd never thought of myself as rich. Scott had a good job, and

I kept the house when we separated. We had decent vehicles, but rich? No way.

I tried again.

"I think what I wanted to say to you—what I want to say—is that my son's life was worth more than a year."

"Who said it was only worth a year?" Hanrahan countered.

"The judge, for one, and you when you smiled at sentencing."

lifted his arm like he was going to scratch his face, but the cuffs prevented it. "How much do you think a life's worth?"

"It depends on whose life we're talking about. Yours? Nothing. A child's? Everything."

"See, that's the truth of it," he said, his voice firm. "That's how you really feel, that I'm a piece of shit. I was a child once, too. You think my life went the way I wanted it to go? It didn't."

He'd always been a monster to me and nothing more. To see him as a human being would be to give in, and to let go of the anger would be to forget my son.

But I was curious.

"Tell me your story," I said.

He studied me hard for a minute. "You're not messin' with me?"

"I'm not."

"Okay…"

His life started with two parents, a younger sister, and a dog named Bob. Then his dad lost his job building rotorcraft parts at Boeing International. The first thing to go was the house, which they sold, and downsized, meaning eight-year-old Jay moved schools and had to say goodbye to friends he'd known since kindergarten. Around this time his mom's behaviour became erratic. She'd always been the marches-to-her-own-drummer type, but it had gotten worse. More extreme. She was either in bed all day or selling their stuff online. One day, Jay got home to an empty house.

She'd sold the couches, kitchen table, and chairs while he was at school.

His dad got a job in a warehouse working nights, but the pay wasn't the same. He was always tired, stressed, and unsure of what to do with his wife. When she disappeared for a two-day stretch, he called emergency services, and they found her ranting in a McDonald's play area about government spies, the flatness of the Earth, and immigration.

Then it got worse.

"I dropped out of high school in grade 11." Hanrahan sniffed. "Did all kinds of shit. Sold drugs. Stole cars. Then I went straight and did carpentry. I always drank, though. Always."

He'd had a tough life, but who hadn't?

I left the room, sat quietly on the couch, and weighed the pros and cons of killing him. I knew I couldn't forgive him.

That's when the doorbell rang.

‡

I gagged Hanrahan, told him to be quiet, and checked the doorbell camera on my phone.

Oh no…

The man standing there was twenty-five or so, thin, and had an army brush cut. He looked like the kind of person who ratted out colleagues when they took an extra long lunch. I read the logo on the breast of his polo: Department of Corrections.

More doorbell.

Hard knocks.

Shit shit shit.

If I didn't answer, he'd just return.

In the kitchen, I loaded the syringe, remembering where to insert it. I forced myself to take deep breaths and held the needle behind my back as I opened the door.

"Hello," I said in my calmest voice.

"Hi," he said pleasantly. "Are you Mara?"

"Yes, how can I help?"

He flashed his credentials, something I could tell he liked doing, and introduced himself as Nate Wamsley, Jay Hanrahan's parole officer.

"Who's Jay Hanrahan?" I said, my right hand on the doorknob, left one hidden.

He smiled like he knew I was lying. "I was at my favorite sandwich joint for lunch, Shifty's Sandwiches, enjoying a BLT on rye, no mayo, and a coffee, reading articles about an accident that occurred almost two years ago. I read about a drunk driver—Jay Hanrahan—running a red light, injuring a patrol, and killing a child. Hanrahan was convicted of dangerous driving. He served a year, but I guess that wasn't enough for you."

The blood vibrated in my veins. "What do you mean?"

My voice sounded weak and puny.

"The boy's name was Cody Rust. Parents, Tim and Mara Rust. That's you," he said, pointing. "There's no delicate way to say this… I know Jay Hanrahan had an appointment at the St. Boniface Clinic on Tuesday night, and he hasn't been seen since then. He's not at home, and he hasn't been to work. What are the chances the man responsible for the death of your son ends up getting an MRI where you work, only to disappear? Wouldn't you agre—"

I swung the door open and pounced, aiming the needle for the exterior of his left thigh, sinking the plunger. He realized what I had done and reached for the needle, but I swiped his hand away until he collapsed on the steps.

‡

Two Weeks Later

The rain pattered the windowpane like fingers made of wood, as kids and their parents braved the inclement weather, screaming 'Trick or Treat,' carrying pillowcases or plastic buckets shaped like pumpkins. The wind swept through the entrance, as I admired my yard. I'd gone all-out this year.

An eight-foot-tall witch sat on the lawn, plugged in, and glowing like a jellyfish.

The trees were covered in fake cobwebs.

Dry ice leaked from the open garage like smoke.

Spooky sound effects emanated from speakers hidden in the garden along the walk.

And the kicker, the cherry on top of an incredible scene, were the men who lay comatose on stretchers on either side of the front entrance, just inside, but far enough away that trick-or-treaters could not know for certain if the men were dummies or real.

I'd given each of them a massive hit of ketamine, and they lay cuffed to their GhostBed Flex Adjustable beds, drooling, eyes rolled back in their sockets.

When a child asked if they were real, I smiled and said, "Of course not."

A group of five kids arrived, screaming for candy without a care in the world. Their laughter echoed in the night as I closed the door and smiled at Hanrahan and Wamsley who lay before me.

My captives. My charges. My children.

Joel Nedecky teaches high school English in Winnipeg, Manitoba. His short stories have appeared in Punk Noir, Guilty Crime Story Magazine, Urban Pigs Press, Hoosier Noir, Shotgun Honey, and Bristol Noir. His debut novel, *The Broken Detective*, will be released by Run Amok Crime in 2025. He is a member of The Manitoba Writers' Guild, as well as Crime Writers of Canada.

The Devil's Rheostat

John Bukowski

The pain blazed white, as if the devil turned a rheostat. The world became the grainy blur of an old sepia photo before swimming back to cold, damp clarity.

"Did you hear me?"

"Huh? What?" Bob gasped.

"I said, move your head," his wife, Sara replied. "You want me to crack your skull open closing the door?"

"Wouldn't be the worst thing to happen to me today," Bob mumbled, inching his head toward his chest. The door slam popped like a gunshot inches from his ears.

"You okay?" Sara asked.

Bob rested his head on the door handle.

"I said, are you…"

"Yes," he shouted louder than he'd intended, immediately regretting the effort that flared his pain to incandescence.

"You don't have to yell."

"Sorry." Clammy sweat beaded his brow and upper lip.

"I'll get somebody from emergency to help you into a wheelchair."

"Leave the engine running," Bob panted. "For the AC."

Her slam of the driver's door tensed his back with another flash of pain. But it was nothing like the agony of moving his legs. And he didn't even want to think about transitioning into a wheelchair.

It had been one of those stupid things that made people with back problems feel just as stupid. He'd leaned over to pull a box from under his workbench. The box had been just heavy enough and the angle just acute enough to zap his lower back. Then the devil twisted that rheostat and Bob couldn't straighten up.

It had taken them fifteen minutes to get him into the back seat. Moving faster than a snail or putting weight (any weight) on his right leg was enough to fray the world into coarse shadows and slimy sweat. Each time, he'd recovered just this side of blacking out, but he didn't think that luck would hold. He knew that sometime soon he'd have to not only move, but transition from horizontal to vertical to seated. The very thought shot spasms. So, he lay stretched across the back seat listening to the rumble of the SUV's engine and feeling sorry for himself.

At least cars still had bench seats in the back, he thought. When he was growing up, benchers were front and back, without the seatbelt posts digging into his flesh right now. Seatbelts were optional then. He smiled at the insanity of safety reduced to an option for the rich. Quite a different world then. His chuckle was rewarded with another spasm.

So, this was how it was going to be. The path forward from sixty-five to…whenever. His spinal X-rays already looked like snow drifting over a ladder. The back pain would become more and more progressive, more and more severe, for longer and longer periods. Disability would follow as surely as death followed life. These acute episodes flat on his back would gradually be replaced by rare moments when he wasn't, moments when upright walking without pain would be was a pleasant surprise. He'd go from cane to walker to wheelchair. He'd have surgeries—vain attempts to make some palliative sense out of the jumble of collapsed discs and arthritic breaks. And it would only get worse.

When you were a kid and broke an arm or sprained an ankle, it was an inconvenience to be borne on the road to "all better." "All better" was a thing of the past. His future would be a "little better" followed by "no better" followed by "worse." Eventually, and not that long really, his life could be described by one word— bedridden. Unless of course, death claimed him first. Not a bad idea, he thought.

Sara tried to understand but couldn't. He thought of her admonition not to shout when shouting was his only release. Younger doctors and physical therapists were likewise unsympathetic; to them, he was an illness, not a person in agony. Even God didn't seem to get it; if the old man really existed, why didn't he end this suffering?

Bob sighed and wiped away a tear. He listened to the AC hum under the rumble of the engine. He heard traffic noise. He heard an errant backfire. Those were sounds of life. Sounds you still heard even as your prospects of life dwindled.

The driver's door opened with a gust of humid summer air. Bob tensed for his pending heroic journey—--the twenty-foot trip from car to admission desk. He hoped they had smelling salts.

"Over here you dumb bitch! The engine's running."

Bob never understood millennials. Not their feelings of entitlement. Not their thin skins. Not their manner of speech. But did emergency-room orderlies talk like this now? This errant thought was cut off by the deluge of pain accompanying slammed doors and rocking car springs. His back spasmed. His world grayed.

"Don't you call me that. I ain't dumb."

"Well, you ain't smart." The car popped into drive. "Didn't I tell you to change out that goddam oil pump?"

"I don't got no goddam money for no goddam oil pump 'cause you smoked it up."

Before Bob could say something clever like, 'Who are you people?' or 'What's going on?' the car lurched forward, Bob's back along with it. His muscles tensed; his teeth clenched.

"Fuckin' getaway car gets a fuckin' warning light and the dumb fuckin' bitch don't say a fuckin' word."

"I did too. I say, 'I hope this goddam car holds out till we ditch it.'"

More waves of pain lanced white as the SUV took a corner way too fast and accelerated even faster.

"And that's supposed to tell me we got us a jacked-up warning light on the goddam engine temperature?"

"Fuck off, Roy!"

"What?"

"Um, nothin."

The car swerved. Bob braced against the front seat to ease the sudden pain. Then he heard a click.

"You gonna apologize for that? Or should I cap your ass right here and get me a new bitch. One who knows enough to fix the fuckin' getaway car."

There was a pause, and then the woman said, "I'm sorry, Sug."

"Damn right, you're sorry. You the sorriest dumb bitch ever lived."

Even as Bob braced against the sudden turns, even as his mind fought against the pain, something was becoming clear. These were not hospital orderlies.

"Shit. What I put the fuck up with." The man paused. "How much we get?" The woman didn't answer. "I said, how much we get, bitch?"

Bob heard the unmistakable sound of shaking pills. "Bottle of oxy and this stuff."

"What stuff?"

She answered hesitantly. "Rob-ax-ham."

"What that?"

"How the hell I supposed to know what that? I ain't no Nurse Jackie nor CSI nor nothin."

"Well, can't you read? What's the label say?"

"Say, 'May cause dizziness. May cause drowsiness.'"

"Okay. Alright. Makes you dizzy. Makes you sleepy. Bound to be some kind of hot shit."

"Also say, 'Take one three times a day for…Look out!'"

The car broke suddenly and swerved. Bob's body followed suit. Agony lanced through Bob's back. He screamed something; he wasn't sure what. The world went dim around the edges, then grayed to a tiny tunnel.

Bob's face flushed. Then he was back inside the moving car, drenched in sweat and listening to the middle of a conversation between a man and woman definitely not in the medical field.

"I said, you trying to get us killed?" the woman said.

"No, no…Before that."

"I didn't say nothin' before that."

"Sounded like 'son of a bitch.' You callin' me a son of a bitch now? Huh?"

The woman sounded panicked. "No, Sug. I didn't call you nothin'."

"Call me that one more time and you gonna get smacked in the cock sucker?"

"I said I didn't call you nothin'."

The car stopped abruptly amidst a squeal of brakes. Bob's body didn't get the memo, so it kept moving, caroming off the front seat and into the foot well. Flashbulb pops turned to stars in Bob's head. Just before he passed out, he heard someone yelling "Dear God!" He thought it might be him.

‡

Bob saw the brown vinyl of the front seat only inches from his eyes. Then he saw the plastic of the SUV's dome light. Between the two was a greasy, pock-marked face partially covered by a scraggly beard. Thin but well-muscled arms emerged from the guy's sleeveless tee shirt. His chapped lips parted, revealing a dingy grin with a blackened eye tooth.

"You okay, old dude?"

Bob didn't know how to answer. He seemed to be in one piece, a piece slickered with sweat.

"What you doin' down there?"

What was he doing down here? Bob wondered.

"This your car?"

Finally, a question he could answer. "Yes."

The greasy face nodded. Another face swam into view; a

mousy girl of nineteen or twenty, who might be considered pretty with a little sunshine and proper diet. She held out a water bottle. "Here. Drink this."

The bottle reached his lips and Bob took a sip. Tepid water dribbled down his chin.

"'Fraid it's warm," the woman said.

"'Course it's warm, you dumb bitch. Been layin' on the dash of a fuckin' car sittin' in the fuckin' sun."

"Stop callin' me dumb…asshole."

A blue-steel revolver pointed at the girl. "What I tell you?"

"Um," Bob said. "Who are you?"

That dingy smile again. "We your friendly neighborhood car thieves. First time with someone in the backseat, though." His face darkened. "What you doin' down there?"

"Back," Bob grunted. Pain ramping up as he spoke. "Back went out on me. My wife was taking me to emergency when…"

The man's smile returned. "When we needed a ride. Nice of her to leave the motor running."

"What we gonna do with him, Roy?" the girl said.

The pock-marked face darkened again, revealing an inner ruthlessness that'd been hidden behind the boyish smile.

"Well, pop? What we gonna do with you? Any thoughts?" Bob watched Roy tap his own chin with the revolver's short barrel. "Cause, I got me one."

"Roy," the woman said softly, as if Bob wasn't supposed to hear. "You can't."

"Yeah?" Roy replied, still smiling down at Bob. "Why not?"

"I have money," Bob said.

Roy's eyebrows rose. "Yeah? Let's see it."

"Not on me. But in the bank, you know? Investments?"

The woman tugged at Roy's tee shirt.

Roy raised the gun. "Hold on, Shanice. Maybe we're onto somethin' here." He pointed the gun at Bob, more for effect than as a threat. "How much we talkin' about? Big picture."

Bob was too flummoxed to lie. "About four million."

Roy whistled. "You livin' large, ain't ya, pops." His swarthy cheeks tensed in concentration. "Your old lady willin' to part with some to get you back? I mean, she's not divorcing you or nothing, is she?"

"She'll pay," Bob grunted.

The pain was singing again. It was as if the sudden fall and loss of consciousness had knocked it to a back burner,; or maybe it had been the gun pointed at his face. But now the pot was simmering, spasms bubbling up at regular intervals. Bob tried to change position to ease the throbbing, but that only dimmed the edges of his vision and got him sweating.

"Hurt pretty bad?" Roy asked.

"Like sin," Bob groaned.

Roy laughed. "That's good. I like that. Like sin." He pointed the gun over his shoulder. "Maybe we got something up here to take the edge off. Shine, get them pills."

Shanice handed Roy two plastic bottles. They were standard containers used by generic drug makers. Bob had handled them daily before he retired.

"Got us some oxy," Roy said. "And this shit here."

"Robaxim," Bob said. "A muscle relaxant."

Roy raised his brows. "You know about this shit? You a pharmacist or something?"

"Veterinarian. Retired."

"Well, well." He smiled at Shanice. "We got us a well-heeled doggy doctor, Shine. What you say to that?"

Bob held out his hand and tried to smile amidst the waves of pain.

"Which one you want?" Roy asked.

"One of each," Bob said.

Roy tapped the gun against the seat. "That how you ask me to do you a big favor?"

Bob cleared his throat. "Please."

Roy smiled. "That's right. You say please." He laid the gun across the seat back, screwed off the caps, then tapped a white pill from each bottle into his hand. He paused, then tapped a second oxy from the bottle. He winked at Bob.

Bob reached out, pain lancing through him at this small effort.

"Hold on, now. Not so fast." Roy pulled his hand away. "I do you a big favor. Give you somethin' you need. You got to promise to get me what I need." He rapped Bob's head with the fist holding the pills.

Pain flared suddenly and unexpectedly. It was as if Roy's knuckles tapped a raw nerve instead of Bob's brow. The dome light blinked out of existence as the world narrowed to a peephole. Then the light was there again above the pock-marked face.

"You promise?"

"Yes," Bob panted. "Anything."

Roy nodded. "Now we got us an understanding. Here you go."

Bob opened his mouth like a baby bird waiting to be fed as Roy dropped the white tabs into the back of his throat.

"Let's have that water, Shine."

The woman held the bottle to Bob's lips. He swallowed painfully, more of the lukewarm liquid dribbling down his chin. The pills felt like ostrich eggs in his throat , but Bob welcomed them just the same.

"Think I'll join ya," Roy said, dumping half a dozen oxycontin into his palm. Shanice held the water bottle toward him, but he pushed it away. He popped the tabs into his mouth and chewed. Smiling down at Bob, Roy said, "I'm an old hand." Then he capped the pill bottles and tossed them to Shanice.

Shanice tugged his tee shirt. "What we gonna do now, Roy?"

Roy kept smiling at Bob. "We gonna call his bitch to set up a money drop."

"But we don't got no cell phone, Sug."

"I have a phone," Bob said.

Roy's brows raised. "Yeah? Let's have it."

Bob reached gently toward his pants pocket. He tried to smile. "I have to move slow. Until the pills take effect."

Roy's smile never dimmed as he picked up the gun. "I can make you move slower."

Bob took a deep breath, then shoved his hand into his pocket. The pain flared, but not too bad. Raising his hips ever so slightly, he was able to get two fingers around the iPhone and pull it free.

Roy snatched it away almost before it had cleared Bob's pocket.

"Sara is number one on speed dial."

Roy slapped the phone onto the seat back then beat it into bits of plastic with the revolver. Shanice screamed. Debris rained onto Bob's face.

"What you do that for?" Shanice yelled.

The rage on Roy's face changed to mild annoyance. He shook his head, still looking at Bob. "And you say you ain't dumb. Ever hear about tracing a cell phone?"

"What?"

Roy grinned at Bob, that hint of ruthlessness behind the smile. "His wife gives the number to the cops; they trace it to us."

"But how we gonna make the call now?"

Roy rolled his eyes; his gesture saying 'dumb bitch' as much as actually saying it. "Payphone. There's still a few. Got one over at the Kwik Mart on third." He continued staring at Bob, as if daring him to say otherwise. Then he pointed the short-barreled piece between Bob's eyes. "What's the number?"

Bob gulped and told him.

"There's a pen and pad in the glove box to write it down," Bob said.

"I'll remember," Roy said. "I ain't no dumb bitch."

⁜

Bob closed his eyes and listened to Roy and Shanice talking outside. The pills had started to work, lulling him into a dreamy haze. The engine still rumbled, AC blowing from the vent, but Shanice had left the door ajar. Bob could follow their conversation, although they spoke low.

"I don't know, Roy."

"What don't you know? I'll be gone maybe twenty minutes. You stay here with the gun and watch him."

"What if he tries something?"

Roy chuckled. "He's old. He's in pain. He's high on oxy. He ain't gonna try nothin."

"What if he does?"

"Then ya smack him on the head with the gat. Damn. I got to tell you everything?"

"Well, well, what if the woman don't pay? What if she got the FBI listening in? What if…"

"What if? What if?" Roy was yelling like a doper on a high.

"What if Jesus comes down and we got us a rapture? Huh? You think the FB-fuckin'-I lives at their house? Ain't been but half an hour since we snatched the drugs. How's the FBI gonna be tapping his phone? Huh?" He paused. In his mind's eye, Bob could see Roy shaking his head. "Dumb bitch."

Bob heard Shanice start to cry. Despite everything, he felt sorry for her.

Roy's voice grew softer, gentler. The voice of a pimp charming a farm girl just off the bus.

"Hey. What's this?" Bob heard a calming shush. "Don't worry. She's gonna pay. I ain't asking for no two million or nothin. Just something quick. Ten, maybe twenty grand. She can get that from the bank, ante up in an hour. She'll be happy to pay to get the old dude back."

There was the sound of snot being sleeved away.

"Then what?"

"Then," Roy said, his voice still soft and soothing. "We drive over to Paris Park—over in the back under the trees."

"And we leave him there and we run. Right? Get out of town while we can. Right?"

Roy chuckled. "You my dumb little bitch, that's for sure. Yeah, we leave him there. But he can call for help, right? Then the cops come, right? He ID us, right? So, I cap him, and we dump the body. Then we head south. Right?"

"But, but…that ain't stealing drugs, Sug." Her voice got so soft that Bob could barely hear. "That's murder."

"What you talkin' about? We puttin' him out of his misery. What they call mercy killing."

"But they come after us for sure for that. We gonna get caught."

"Nah, we'll never get caught. How we gonna get caught?"

"But, but…"

"Shhh. You leave it to me, baby."

Bob froze. He didn't feel any back pain. He didn't feel the warm mussiness of the drugs. He didn't feel anything but cold realization. The truth had finally sunk in. This wasn't going to end well.

Just a half hour ago—thirty minutes—Bob had been contemplating the horrors of a life with a disability. Thirty minutes ago, death hadn't seemed like such a bad idea. Now, he had only one thought, one prevailing, overriding desire. Life. He wanted the joy of life. He wanted the pain of life. He wanted the horrors of life. All of it. Life under any terms. Walking with a cane was still walking. There was still music, books, movies, food, drink. There were enchiladas, cold beer, and the sharp tang of good bourbon. The sun shone. The stars twinkled. Winter wind was crisp and cold. Birds still sang in the warm summer breeze. Leaves still turned crimson and gold in the autumn, the air tangy with their mustiness. Most of all, Sara still smiled. She was there to talk with. To sleep with. To grow old with. To love.

Escape. He had to get away. But how? The pills helped the pain, he could now move without agony. But could he fight off a young dope addict? He didn't even know if he could stand. And they had a gun. And there were two of them. It seemed hopeless.

Bob heard the unmistakable smack of a kiss. For a few seconds, he didn't hear anything. Then the front door popped, and the car rocked with someone getting in. Then Shanice looked down at him. She held the gun against the headrest, her other hand clutching the seat back. She wasn't smiling.

"Where's your friend?" Bob asked.

"Roy went to call your wife. Get us the money. Then,

um…then we take you to the park. Let you go."

"Is that right?"

Bob fought the urge to beg for his life. To tell Shanice about Sara. Appeal to her humanity. Say he'd send them the money. Anything to convince her to let him go before Roy came back. But she trusted Roy, not Bob. She probably even feared Roy. No, Bob didn't think she'd care about his troubles, his wife, his life. And it would give away his edge, his ace in the hole. She'd know he'd overheard.

"Yeah. That right. So just relax and let the pills do your pain. You want more water?"

He tried to smile despite the hard knot twisting his gut. "No. I'll just have to pee, and I don't feel like doing it in my pants in the back of a car."

Shanice smiled back. She had a nice smile. Bob imagined that smile in a high -school yearbook. Maybe leading the pep squad or as treasurer of the Spanish club. But he doubted she'd been a cheerleader or estudiante de español. Her Spanish was probably limited to puta, mierda, and cabróon. Words picked up on the street, just as she'd been picked up by Roy. On the street. No graduation day, no prom night. When had it started? At sixteen? Fifteen? Dumb bitch, Bob thought. But was she?

She'd been smart enough to be against killing. She knew that stealing drugs was one thing; murder was a whole new shitstorm. Lethal injection in this state. And maybe she was against killing, morally against it. Yeah, maybe she wasn't as bad as Roy. Maybe she wasn't so dumb either. And she didn't like being called dumb. That could be an angle, a tool he could use. Bob felt a ray of hope. He swallowed hard.

"So, you're just going to let me go in the park, huh?"

"Yeah. Sure. Um, what we want to keep you for? We get the

money. We let you go."

"Aren't you afraid I'll talk to the cops? I've seen your faces. I know your names."

She didn't say anything. She just stared at him, not knowing what to say or do.

"I bet that Roy doesn't want to just let me go. Right?"

Shanice flinched. Perhaps she got an inkling that Bob had overheard. Perhaps it was just hearing him say right the way she and Roy had.

"How did you get hooked up with a guy like Roy in the first place, Shanice? Smart kid like you. I figured you for college. Maybe a job in a dental office."

She laughed. It was a nice laugh, musical. "College? Shit. I ain't even finished high school."

"That's no problem. You could get a GED. High school equivalency." Prisoners earned them all the time, he thought but didn't say. "Wouldn't take long. Smart girl like you. Maybe get a part-time job. Go to community college. You'd be working for that dentist before you know it."

She looked at him more in surprise than anything else. Bob wondered if she had ever imagined a future like that. Or if anyone had ever imagined it for her. He felt angry that they hadn't.

"Beats blowing out birthday candles in Coleman for thirty years," Bob said. "That's a federal prison. Tough time."

"What you talking about, federal?"

Bob nodded. There was no pain now. "Kidnapping is a federal crime. Thirty-year maximum. But you might get a sympathetic judge. Only do five or ten. Of course…"

"Course what?"

"Premeditated murder is a capital crime." Bob mimicked a

syringe in the arm. "They give you the needle for that."

"You crazy. I said we gonna let you go. We ain't dumb enough to go down on no murder rap."

Bob smiled. He was reaching her. "Maybe you're not. But is Roy?"

"Roy ain't dumb. He smart. He knows things."

"He's a junkie, Shanice. Right now, he's high on oxy and not thinking straight. Not like you. You know murder is a one-way ticket to the death house."

"Stop saying we gonna kill you! I said we ain't gonna kill you."

"And you know that the law doesn't care who pulls the trigger." He saw surprise in her pretty, dark eyes. "And you know you'll never get away with it."

"Shut up! We won't get caught. Roy smart. He knows stuff. Knows about cell phones and shit."

"Yeah, he knows shit. I bet he picked it up in prison." Bob paused for effect. "He's gotten caught before. Right?"

She looked at him, eyes wide. Bob saw fear behind those eyes. Fear of getting caught. Fear of Roy. Fear of being an accomplice to murder. Fear of a new, dark, terminal path in her young life. Bob felt pity for her. He wanted to get to know her, comfort her. But he didn't have the luxury of time. In twenty minutes, maybe less, she would no longer be in control. Bob had to make good use of the now.

"Shanice," he said, his voice soft and understanding. "You're with a junkie who's got a record. You're traveling in a stolen car. People saw you at the hospital. Now you're involved in kidnapping and murder." He reached up and laid his hand on hers. He felt her shiver. "Do you really think you'll get away with it?"

She sat still for a moment, her hand trembling under his, her wide eyes glistening. Then she jerked her hand away and turned toward the windshield.

"Shit," she said, wiping her nose with her gun hand. "We was just gonna grab some drugs from the e room. They got a cart there, just inside the glass. Keep pills in it. So they don't got to run back and forth to the drug room I guess." She turned back, her face animated. "I seen it last month. Roy hurt my…I mean, I hurt my hand." She held up the gun and twisted her wrist. "Thought it was busted. Turned out was just a sprain. But I seen 'em go to that cart and take out the pain pills they give me. Just six, but they took them from that bigger bottle."

"And you told Roy," Bob said.

She nodded. "He say, he go first and distract the lady at the desk. Then I come in and say I got some belly problem. I act real sick. Scream. Make a fuss. When they run over to see about me, Roy step in and snatch a bottle out of the cart."

"And is that what happened?"

"Shit. Before I even start screaming, Roy pops a cap into the safety glass."

Bob remembered hearing what he thought was a backfire earlier.

"Then I start screamin'. Everybody start screamin'. Roy start screamin' for everybody to shut the fuck up."

"So, you grabbed the drugs and ran?"

"First Roy lay the gun over some nurse's head. She falls to the floor and start bleeding. Then he point the gun at another one and say, "You wanna play, bitch?" He thumb back the hammer. I thought he was gonna shoot."

"What did you do?"

"I grabbed inside the cart, snatched the two bottles, then grabbed him. I say, I got it, Roy. Let's go."

"And he went? Just like that?"

She shook her head. She wanted to tell it now. Get it off her chest or just explain to another person. So that another living soul would understand how she came to be sitting there with a gun waiting for a boyfriend who beat her and was going to make her an accomplice to murder. Bob again felt sorry for her. He found himself liking her. She was easy to like. Just as Roy was easy to hate. He hated Roy for many reasons, but right now, this second, Bob hated Roy for what he was doing to Shanice.

"No," she said. "He keep smiling at this nurse standin' there, bout to pee her pants. Keeps pointing the gun in her face. Finger on the trigger. I shook his other arm, one not holding the gun, and say, '"Cops be coming. We gotta go."' Her face went cold. "He stop smiling. Like…"

"He was disappointed?"

Shanice nodded.

"Then you left?"

She shook again. Her hair was frizzled, and dry, but clean. Her overall appearance suggested her personal hygiene was better than her boyfriend's. No greasy hair, no pimply face.

"He pointed the gun at me, finger tight on the trigger." Bob could see the terror in her eyes at the recollection. Her throat bobbed with a hard swallow. "Then he smiled at me. Then we went."

"But the car conked out on you. Huh?"

"I left the motor runnin', just like he say. Wasn't my fault that damn oil pump decide to die." She laid the gun on the seat back and wiped her eyes.

"You saved that woman's life, Shanice."

"Huh?"

"That nurse? The one he pointed the gun at. He was going to kill her. Like he thought about killing you. Like he's planning on killing me."

Shanice just stared at him, teary eyes wide with relived memories and future fears.

"You know he was going to kill her." Her eyes said she did indeed know. "You stopped him. You saved her life."

Bob saw the gun from the corner of his eye. It lay unattended and forgotten atop the vinyl of the front seat, its blued metal glistening with oil and Shanice's sweat. He didn't look directly at it. Instead, he spoke to her.

"That was very brave. He could have killed you for it. He almost did."

She looked at him, jaw open. He could see she knew it was true.

"That's what they call an extenuating circumstance, Shanice. The kind of thing that judges take into consideration when passing sentence."

She shook her head, as if coming out of a trance. "No. Roy wouldn't have done nothin' to me."

"Like he didn't do anything to your wrist?"

She looked down at him and blinked. Then she started to say something, but no words came out.

"Like he didn't do anything to the nurse he conked over the head." She opened her mouth again but still made no sound. "He could have killed her too, Shanice."

She turned away, again wiping her eyes. "No, he just gave her a tap. He wouldn't a killed her."

"He's going to kill me, Shanice."

Her neck snapped over to look at him. This time, she didn't try to deny it. "You heard him, huh?"

"Yes, Shanice. I heard him say he was going to murder me."

She continued staring down at him from over the front seat, her hands gripping the vinyl, the gun balanced nearby.

"He's a murderer, Shanice. And he's going to make you a murderer, too."

A tear rolled down her cheek.

"Worse yet. You'll be a witness."

Another tear joined the first.

"The sole witness to murder."

Realization finally lit her face. A realization she hadn't considered—or had denied.

"I don't think Roy likes witnesses, Shanice." Bob laid his hand over hers. He patted gently. "I think he gets rid of them." Then he slid his hand toward the gun.

Her eyes followed his hand, a jumble of confused emotions in them. But she didn't move.

"I think he kills them."

Bob laid his hand atop the blued steel. It was cold and hard. It felt like death. Shanice watched, eyes fixed, a snake coiled and ready. But she didn't strike.

"You're not a person to him, Shanice." Bob clasped the pistol's grip, adding his sweat to hers. "You're a thing. A thing to be used."

Still, she watched but didn't move.

He tightened his grip, feeling the give of the hard rubber. "Used for sex. Used to get him drugs. Used to vent his frustrations on."

She clutched her wrist.

"Just a thing, Shanice." Bob slid the pistol toward him. "Just a dumb bitch." He pulled the revolver to his chest.

Shanice continued to stare, her body a coiled spring unsure of release. Then she blinked. Her shoulders sank. Her frame relaxed. She sighed.

Bob could see the relief in her. The decision was made. That new, strange, dangerous path was closing down. Perhaps she would remain free. Perhaps alive.

Bob reached behind his head (there was still no pain) and pushed the window button. He heard the soft hum as it descended. He felt a gust of warm air; it smelled sweet and clean with a hint of new-cut grass. It smelled like summer. It smelled like life. Bob lifted the gun and pointed it at Shanice. She stared but didn't move. Then he tossed it over his head and out the open window.

Bob heard the clunk of metal on pavement. "Drive me to the hospital, Shanice. I think I can make it to the door on my own now." Then he answered the question her eyes were asking. "Then you drive away and find a new life. A life away from Roy."

She stared, mouth open. Then she smiled.

"A life away from Roy, huh?"

Bob flinched at the new voice, the voice behind the gun pointing at him through the open window. Roy was smiling down as well, the smile that didn't quite hide the true evil of the man. "Cat be away, and the mice will play, huh?"

"Hey, Sug," Shanice shouted. "It ain't what you think. He grab the…" The gun pointed her way and she shut up.

"He grab the… the what?" Shanice stammered something unintelligible. "Huh? The gun? This gun?"

Roy's voice rose with each question. Bob watched the man's grip tighten on the handle, his finger on the trigger. Bob knew he was dead. He knew Shanice was dead. He figured she knew it, too.

"Huh? How'd he grab the gun? Huh?" The gun shook with rage. "You dumb bitch." This last was spoken calmly, as if it was common knowledge of no real importance. Then a bit of the manipulative pimp came back into Roy's voice. "I was gonna take you with me, Shine. We was gonna take the money we got and live large. But now…" Bob watched Roy thumb back the hammer. He heard the click as it seated in the killing position. Roy's finger tensed on the trigger.

Shanice would soon be dead. Bob knew this as surely as he knew the sun would rise tomorrow. As surely as he knew he would not be there to see that sunrise. It was now or never.

Bob reached up and grabbed Roy's wrist. He didn't think about it. Thinking would be as deadly to him as Roy. He just did it. Bob didn't think about his next move either. He let his reflexes take over. It was like a knee-jerk, an ingrained response that bypassed his brain.

Bob gripped Roy's wrist with both his hands. He felt hard bone. He felt clammy sweat over dark, greasy hairs. He felt Roy's pulse hammering. The man is as scared as I am, Bob thought. The thought gave him hope.

Bob's pain had disappeared, although a part of him knew that it would eventually be back. No time to think about that now. Such thinking would get him killed. Now was the time for survival. The time for adrenaline. Fight or flight…or death.

Bob forced Roy's gun hand toward the back window. His kidnapper had positioned himself toward the rear of the car, in order to better point the gun at Shanice, so there was really no place for his arm to go. As Roy's bicep struck the door frame, Bob kept pushing, overextending the elbow. Roy screamed. The gun fired once, blowing out the side window. Bob's ears rang with a sharp, metallic ping; the flash blinded him. When his vision returned, he saw the pistol bouncing onto the rear seat.

Now what? Bob had time for this one conscious thought before he was back in reflex, adrenaline mode.

His adversary hadn't been incapacitated for long. As Bob held on, forcing the gun hand further, trying to break the elbow, the junkie's other hand shot through the window and grabbed Bob's neck.

Bob recalled handling owls and hawks during vet school, the pressure of the talons as they fought to penetrate the heavy leather gloves to the human flesh below. Roy's grip was like that. Despite the narcotic in Bob's system, the pain was as intense as dropping a barbell on your throat. Bob knew on a subliminal level that the pain in Roy's elbow must be almost as bad. But the other man was several decades younger and had a lot more oxy in his system. There was really no question as to who would break first. After several seconds, Bob did.

Bob released his grip on one wrist and latched both hands onto the wrist that was choking the life from him. It felt like gripping a radiator pipe. Above him, he saw Roy's evil grin return as the junkie's other hand joined the first. Bob hammered vainly against the wrists choking him. The end was inevitable now.

Roy's hands squeezed. Bob beat against them and strained to suck in air, even a little that might ease the burning in his chest. The world turned gray, feathering around the edges just as it had with the worst of his back pain. But this time, there would be no trip to the ER. Soon things would telescope into a small, dark tunnel. Then he would black out. Then he'd be headed to the morgue.

Bob couldn't think. His mind only registered a kaleidoscopic series of memories. Chipping his front teeth when he was twelve. Confirmation mass with Bishop Schrock. His first driving lesson, his dad's yell when he bumped the Buick over the curb. Feeling up Rebecca Samuels in that very same Buick. Meeting Sara at a vet school party, her hair glistening in the bonfire light. Sara in her wedding dress. Their honeymoon. An errant thought fought its way upstream, maybe the last thought he'd ever have. Your life really did pass before your eyes.

Bob closed his eyes. He was no longer much of a Catholic—hadn't attended mass in years. But its ritual still hid within the recesses of his brain. The words arose now as if on a teleprompter. Oh my God. I am heartily sorry for having offended thee. I detest all my sins…Oh dear God, help me.

Suddenly the car lurched forward. The pressure around Bob's throat vanished and he could breathe—large, heaving, heavenly gasps. His graying vision flashed bright, then returned to normal. He saw Roy's eyes widen in surprise as they slid below the open window.

Bob sat up, ignoring the returning spasm in his back. He looked over the console and saw Shanice driving, her determined expression in the rearview mirror. Then Bob heard a scream, a wail not unlike a dog being run over by a car. There was a thump as the SUV sped atop something. The screaming stopped mid-wail. .

Bob glanced again in the rearview and saw Roy. It was a distant image, one quite different from the wired-up junkie with an evil smile. This Roy lay still on the pavement, his belly flat as a wasp's, a tire track across it.

The car sped down the road and through a stop sign.

"Better watch your driving, Shanice." Bob's voice was a gravely mumble, but she must have heard. The car slowed.

"How's your back?" she asked.

"I'll live," Bob replied. She smiled at him in the rearview. "Where are we going?"

"I'm taking you to the hospital," she said calmly.

"And then?"

Her smile dimmed. "Then…Then I guess I be going to jail."

Bob reached out to pat her shoulder. "Maybe not. I can get you a good lawyer." He lay back down. "Even help you with that GED." Scenes of life flashed by the window. "God willing, maybe help you with a lot of things."

John Bukowski was previously a researcher and medical writer with professional publications ranging from journal articles to website content to radio scripts. In fiction, he has two novels, *Project Suicide* and *Checkout Time,* and seventeen short stories in publication. He's a native of the Midwest, but currently lives in eastern Tennessee.

Therefore I Am

Ken Sparrow

I can hear it now, the husk that slowly
climbs the stairs that ascend to the hallway
outside my bedroom door. The floorboards creak
as it reaches the top and I picture it, standing just
outside. I shiver under my covers, hugging my
pillow to my chest, but it affords little comfort.
Alone, I wait.

The doorknob turns and it enters.

"All ready for bed?" it asks.

I nod in the affirmative.

It moves to the side of the bed and leans
down, hovering over me. Its dead eyes search
my face, trying to find me where I hide inside.

"Are you feeling ok, baby?"

Again, I nod.

"Do you need anything?"

I can almost hear the gears turning deep inside the mother-thing, making it speak, and I shake my head, no.

"Sebastian, remember what Dr. Elliot said; you need to use your words."

Dr. Elliot. Prematurely bald and hollow-cheeked. Endlessly condescending. The one that calls me "special," "gifted," and "intelligent far beyond my ten years" all while feigning understanding, and worse, concern. The one that questions everything. The one that records everything. I made the mistake of answering it honestly once, and now they watch me closely.

The mother-thing speaks again.

"I love you, Sebi."

It's just part of the ritual, the call and response, and if I answer, it will leave that much sooner. But there is something else in its voice tonight, something so close to real that it makes me question myself.

I look into its eyes, searching for a glimmer. Are you in there? Do you see me? Perhaps something looked back, but I can't be certain.

I roll over and face the wall. It continues to stand there for a time, then sighs and moves off, turning out the light and closing the door behind it before descending the stairs, going back from whence it came.

I lay in the dark, thinking of the night, months ago, when I woke from the dream.

3:34 AM by the red light of my alarm clock, I sat bolt upright, soaked in sweat, seeing the world for the first time. I existed. I was here, and this was happening. I, was happening. I was the voice in my head;, the speaker and the listener. I was alone, trapped inside, and I could not escape. Not ever. I rolled over and vomited into my wastebasket, choking on bits of half-digested meatloaf and peas.

It was at that exact moment, head hanging over the side of my bed, coughing and struggling to breathe, that the terrible thought first occurred to me.

What about the others?

Were they like me, trapped inside, prisoners of their own perspective, or was I the only one? What if I was all there was, the only watcher of a play put on just for me? What if I was all alone in the entirety of the universe?

I vomited again and again until my sides ached, and my throat burned with the taste of bile. I hid, shivering under the covers until I fell asleep, exhausted.

They came in the next morning, the mother-thing and the father-thing, expressing their surprise and concern. The reeking trash can was whisked away, and the filthy sheets were pulled from the bed. A great show was made, searching for signs of fever.

I did not leave my bed for three days.

A parade of doctors followed. They examined me for traces of infection and shadows of the brain, and as they did, I watched them back, hunting for signs of sentience. They went about their work, as busy as ants, but did they know it? Were they aware? And if they did, how would I know?

The solution eluded me, and I withdrew. What was the point of speaking to these things if there was no one there to hear me? Soon after, they introduced Dr. Elliot.

Intensive therapy, they called it. Daily sessions. They wore me down with endless words, question after question, and in a desperate attempt to make it stop, I finally expressed my fear.

It was then the pills started.

For a time, they helped, at least insofar as they made me like the others, empty and unaware. Time passed, unobserved. Perhaps there was fear, but if there was, it wasn't mine. I don't remember deciding to stop taking them, but the decision was made, and now, for the second time, I am awake.

With my newfound clarity, the solution is suddenly obvious, so obvious that I don't know why I didn't think of it before. Philosophical questions require empirical solutions. Indisputable evidence of what is and what is not. I once read of a Zen monk, a student, who proclaimed to his master that the world did not exist. The Zen master simply smiled and slapped the student across the face.

If I am not alone, others must exist. If others exist, they can be found. But first I must gather my tools.

I start with the sister-thing that sleeps in the room across the hall, using a hammer to crack it open like a walnut while it lies breathing softly in bed. It is my first attempt, and the mess is terrible. Gouts of blood paint the walls and soak the comforter, blending together the small red hearts printed on it. Inside I see nothing obvious, no clear sign, but I am thorough and work my fingers through the contents just in case. In the end, I am neither surprised nor disappointed that it is empty.

The father-thing is next. I find it on the couch in the family room, where it has been sleeping as of late. A light tap of the hammer is all it takes to drive the Phillips head screwdriver into the eye socket all the way up to its black and yellow handle. The thing on the couch flails about like a fish on a hook and then is still. It was likely no more aware of its demise than it was of anything else it encountered as it moved through this world. Unless I was wrong about it. I need to look inside to be sure. The coping saw makes quick work of it and there is surprisingly little blood this time. When I finally finish my examination, I place the top of the skull on the coffee table, where it sits like a bowl of bean dip. There was nothing to find in this one either and I wonder if perhaps I made a mistake. I ponder it for a few minutes, twirling the screwdriver in my fingers until suddenly the answer is clear.

How can there be awareness without consciousness?!

I quickly gather my tools and walk down the hall to the mother-thing's room. I make no effort to be stealthy, I am not Dr. Elliot's only patient, and the mother-thing has pills of its own. The zip ties are firmly in place, and I am nearly ready to begin before it even stirs from its medicated slumber. I slap it fully awake and quickly jam a knotted rag in its mouth, tying it tightly behind its head. The neighbor's house is far too distant for anyone to hear it scream, but I don't want the distraction.

This time I work slowly, methodically peeling back one layer at a time. If there is a homunculus within, it will not escape my notice. I am forced to stop several times during the night to secure the mother- thing more tightly. It is stronger than it appears. It writhes and strains against its bonds, its muted screams rising with the growing intensity of my exploration.

Eventually, it falls silent, and shortly after, it ceases to even twitch. I am forced to accept that this one too—the one I most hoped would be different—was nothing more than an automaton, and I am still alone.

I write these words for you, if you exist, somewhere out there in the dark. If you are reading them, looking out, aware and trapped within, floating lost at the center of your own universe, I want you to know this: we are the same, you and I. You need not despair, nor fear the emptiness anymore, for you are not alone. I am here, as you are, wandering amongst the empty husks. I am here, and I will never stop searching.

I am here, and one day, I will find you.

Ken Sparrow is the author of the short story "Waiting for the Cat to Die", accepted for publication in *Dark Speculations Volume 2*, (expected publication date: October, 31 2025). His novella, *Fern Spike*, was a finalist for the 2024 The William Faulkner - William Wisdom Creative Writing Competition and also received praise from the early reading team of the Master Review 2023-2024 Winter Short Story Award for New Writers. When not writing, Ken spends most of his time in service to our robot overlords working as an electromechanical and software systems engineer. An endurance athlete and avid outdoorsman, Ken finds his imagination most active while cycling and hiking in the woods near his home in coastal Massachusetts, where he sleeps standing up in a closet wearing a tinfoil hat.

BAD CALL

Brian Silverman

The bar was on the Jersey side, just over the Bayonne Bridge. Before crossing the bridge, and still in Staten Island, Sal Machado tossed his chest protector, knee pads, mask, and the dark blue XXL polo shirt with the AYBL logo, into a landfill off the highway. The blue uniform pants and white undershirt, speckled with blood, he kept on for now. His Dodge Ram truck with the blue tinted American flag sticker in support of the police was parked outside the bar. He knew his license plate and the dent in the rear would make it very easy to find him. He thought about ditching the truck, taking a train or a bus somewhere, going on the run, but decided against it. What he needed now were a couple of drinks and to ponder his next move.

It was a late, hot summer Sunday afternoon. Most folks, Sal thought, would be at the beach or picnics; doing stress-free stuff with their families and friends. Not him. He could have done something else to make extra money. He could have worked security somewhere to supplement his corrections officer union salary. But Sal chose to umpire youth baseball games. There were games and tournaments from March through October. He was never lacking for work, but it meant he had to listen to the whining of parents who bought into the fantasy that their babies were budding baseball superstars. Before he got into it, he actually thought he would enjoy being out on the fields and, especially since he had no children, hearing the chatter of boys in dugouts instead of inside the dreary confines of the correctional facility he worked at in Queens. It didn't take him long to realize handling degenerate convicts was in many ways easier than dealing with brats and their psycho parents.

Merengue music was blasting inside the bar. The place was dark and cool—Sal was happy about that. He wasn't so happy about the loud music. The name of the place was The Shamrock and there was a four-leaf clover in neon in the window. He expected a burly Irish bartender and some quiet old drinkers who knew how to mind their business. The few customers turned to look at him as he entered. They weren't old and they weren't quiet. They were yakking in Spanish with the lanky bartender who had a shaved head, tattoos on his neck,and piercings in his ears and nose. Before he even took a seat at the bar, one of the men sitting at the bar, a skinny guy with hair shaved on one side and long and stringy on the other, pointed to him. "There's Nestor," he said with a smirk.

Sal took a deep breath and sat, ignoring whatever the hell the dude meant by "There's Nestor."

The bartender came over, said nothing, waited.

"Four Roses," Sal said, and added "neat," avoiding eye contact. That was the idea—avoid eye contact. Or any contact at all.

"Hey, Nestor. How many strikeouts today?" The skinny guy asked.

Again, Sal ignored him.

"Come on, Nestor. How you do?"

"Nestor?" Machado asked, finally looking the skinny guy in the eye.

"Yeah, yeah. Nestor." He pointed to Sal's mustache. It was very dark almost as if it was dyed. "Ain't you, Nestor the pitcher on the Yankees?"

"You got the wrong guy," Sal said and downed the Four Roses. He tapped the shot glass for another. The bartender filled the glass.

"No, you the right guy." And then the skinny guy started giggling and laughing.

Sal shook his head, said nothing, and stared up at the game show playing on the television. The show was in Spanish and there were no subtitles. He didn't know what was going on, but it looked like they were having fun. Sal had a Cuban father and an Italian mother, but he didn't speak either Spanish or Italian, and neither did they. With his swarthy complexion, this wasn't the first time he was mistaken for being Hispanic—Latino—Spanish—whatever the right term these days. He even got mistaken for an Arab a few times. There were a few of the correction officers, hard-ass bigots from Long Island who would kid him and call him "Habibi." He had to look up what that meant. He didn't get into it with them. He had to co-exist. He had to show restraint. That was what he was taught as a corrections officer, and before that in the army. And now also as a youth baseball umpire. So the dude calling him Nestor, mistaking him for someone else, wasn't a complete shock. It was just something he didn't want to hear now.

"Nestor, how many strikeouts," he asked. The skinny dude had his face now right up in Sal's. When an inmate got up in his face, Sal did his best to display calm. That usually got the prick to back down. Sal knew his stoic look, and muscular frame, could be intimidating. He understood that the skinny dude was inebriated— he could smell the beer on him. But that was no excuse for getting in his face. And that restraint he was so good at displaying…that was history. He didn't have to show any now. So, he thought, why not?

✝

The motel was off Highway 76 near Reading, Pennsylvania. When he registered, he had to write in the make and license number of his vehicle. He thought about making one up but didn't bother.

His room was on the second floor. He noticed dirty boots

outside many of the doors—the hotel, he surmised, was used to house day workers. And from inside his room, he could hear chattering in Spanish from next door. The view from his window was of a Sheetz gas station. He sat staring at the pumps as cars pulled up to them. He watched as people got out and filled their cars, one after the other. He put his hand in the pocket looking for his phone. But there was nothing there. He remembered that he tossed it after leaving the bar in Bayonne, crushing it under his truck's tires. Word got out fast. It had started buzzing as soon as he left the field in Staten Island. He was sure there was video of what went down there. It didn't matter. He didn't need to see what he had done. Earlier he felt nauseous, but now he was suddenly hungry and sleepy.

He fooled with the room's clock/radio and set the alarm to go off in an hour. He lay down and closed his eyes. He fell asleep immediately and—in what seemed like minutes—the radio came on. He was groggy, didn't know where he was. It was dark now. There were red and white lights outside his window. Sal wondered if they had found him and were out there waiting. He slowly got up from the bed and went to the window. The lights were from the Sheetz station and the numerous cars and their brake lights. He didn't see flashing police lights.

He only had the clothes he wore before he put his umpire uniform on: jeans and a black t-shirt. After a quick shower, he put them on and left the room. Instead of taking the truck, he walked on the sidewalk alongside US 222. Traffic hummed past at a frenetic pace. There were strip malls with fast food drive-thrus, smoke shops, and dollar stores. He didn't know where he was going, but walking felt good and the drone of constant traffic noise seemed to calm him. Sal was not a tall man but was an avid weight lifter. He couldn't explain why, but he liked to show off his bulk in tight shirts. It was seen as a joke at work. The other guards would mock him for showing off, like he was compensating or something. The inmates also. Maybe he hoped his muscles would intimidate them, but it had the opposite effect. They would try him and he had to restrain himself. But not always. There were those few exceptions when a line was crossed and he could shatter a jaw, nose, or rib. He just couldn't do it all the time. He found those rare moments gratifying—cathartic, but he wasn't sure why.

After walking about a mile, he turned into a strip mall and saw a restaurant. There was a red neon sign of a roasted chicken in the window. Peering inside, he saw that customers were scarce. That's what he wanted. He had no idea what kind of restaurant it was but that didn't matter. He sat at a table near the window with a view of 222. A waitress came to his table. She had long dark hair in a ponytail and was wearing a yellow polo shirt and jeans. "Hola," she said with a friendly smile and handed him a plastic laminated menu. He looked at her and then the menu. It was in Spanish.

"No habla," he said to her, hoping she got the idea.

She looked him over, her eyes gazing at his hand that held the menu. His knuckles were red and scabbed fresh with blood. He saw what she was looking at. He didn't try to hide it.

"I speak English. It okay." She gave him one of those friendly smiles again as she looked away from his bruised knuckles. Something smelled very good coming from the restaurant's kitchen. "Drink?"

"Water is fine."

While she went to get his water, he glanced at the menu. He liked the Peruvian chicken he got on Northern Boulevard not far from where he worked. Maybe they had something like that in this place. He hadn't eaten since morning.

"You got that good roast chicken that comes with the rice and beans?" he asked her when she returned.

"Pollo a la brasa?"

Even when she was asking him a question she had that smile. Her teeth were gleaming white, but crooked. Her nose was long and pointed. She wasn't a beauty, but that smile made up for any flaws she had. He could get addicted to it.

"Is that the good chicken?"

"Everybody like pollo a la brasa." She said.

"Okay. Bring it," he said.

She kind of laughed at him and shuffled off. He noticed she was very slender. The jeans she wore were not tight on her bottom like most were on women these days. He wondered if she was just skinny or preferred her jeans not showing off her ass. He also wondered what she would say if he asked her what time she got off from work. Once he finished that chicken, which was as good as what he had on Northern Boulevard, and brought him his check, he learned from her that the restaurant was about to close. He asked if she needed a ride home. Without any hesitation, she said, "Si…please."

While he waited for her outside, a black Challenger pulled up into a spot right in front of the restaurant. He watched as she emerged from the restaurant. He saw her glance at the Challenger that had black-out windows in the front and back and was idling. She nodded at it and then turned to him giving him one of those smiles. "Where the car?" she asked.

"I didn't drive it here. My truck's not far. Do you want to walk?"

"Walk?" She frowned.

"It's not that far," he offered. "We get there and I'll drive you home."

She wasn't moving yet. He didn't know why. And then she just shrugged. He took that as some sort of compliance. As they left the strip mall parking lot, he noticed her turn back to look at the black Challenger. It was pulling out of the parking space. He wondered about that as they walked to the sidewalk. Over the din of the traffic flying past them he asked: "Are you from Mexico?"

"Mexico?" She made a sour face. "No. Venezuela."

He nodded and regretted assuming she was Mexican. He realized he might have insulted her even if he wasn't sure why. "How long have you been here?"

"Five months, I think."

"Must have been tough to leave your family and your country like that?"

She didn't say anything. They were quiet after that as they walked, both of them just moving forward to something.

They came to the hotel parking lot. He pointed to his truck. "It's right there."

She looked up at him and then turned from him. She saw, as he did, the black Challenger enter the motel parking lot. "Now? You want to talk more before we go?" she asked.

"Talk?"

"Yes. In your room?" She kept glancing back at the Challenger.

He didn't want it to go like this. He liked her smile and thought it was sincere. Now he wasn't so sure. He felt her take his hand. It was warm and damp. He looked at her and could see the desperation. "Okay, we'll talk."

He opened the door to his room, turned on a light, and let her in. He locked the door behind them. She sat on one of the double beds. He sat on the other facing her.

"What happen to your hand?" She pointed to his red, blood-dried knuckles.

He didn't tell her that was why he was where he was. She wouldn't understand what he did. And why he did it. He didn't even really understand what happened, or what set him off. He hadn't had the chance to process it all and wasn't sure if he ever would.

✢

It began before he even took his place behind the plate. The sun was already blazing and there was no shade to be found near the Staten Island field. "You gonna get a call right today?" Sal heard from behind the backstop. He recognized the voice—raspy, perpetually hoarse and high-pitched. A sewage stench, he noticed, was coming from New Jersey—wafting over Arthur Kill.

He didn't turn to look back to see who was yapping at him, but he knew. He recognized the voice and if he did turn, he would see the familiar buzz cut of dark hair and the prominent bushy eyebrows above bulging eyes. The man was a parent of one of the sixteen-year-olds playing and was starting in on him as he did a few weeks back at a tournament in Long Island. Every close call made, ball or strike, was questioned. And not only questioned, but mocked. Sal understood that in the role he played as umpire, he would get heat. He was used to it. He couldn't engage.

"Of all the umps, we had to get Osama."

"I think he looks more like Saddam." Someone else, a sidekick, said with a snicker.

He could ignore that bullshit. The joke was on them. He saw enough of their fat asses to see they were probably Italian, or half-Italian, just like him. Idiots.

The first couple of innings went by without incident. There were a few remarks, but nothing more than he was used to.

Between innings, Sal would go get his water, his mask off, and glance at them. The one with the raspy voice kept grinning, taunting him. Sal regretted making eye contact. After that, the remarks were relentless. Every call. "Where was that pitch? That's a ball? That was a strike? Can you get one call right?"

The game was tight. And in sixteen-year-old travel baseball, a tight game meant parents on edge. They took this seriously, convinced Junior was certain to get a scholarship to LSU or Stanford. A short, chunky kid who was a decent third baseman, but not much of a hitter, was up. He knew by now that his father was the asshole behind the backstop. He had nothing against the kid. Sal felt bad for him, actually. Who wants a father like that? When he came up to the plate with a runner on third, two outs, and the game tied, Sal could feel the tension flowing off the poor kid. The first pitch was right down the middle. Sal put up his right finger. "Strike one."

"You let that one go? You'll never get another like that one," he heard his father say. "Now you're screwed with Saddam calling balls and strikes."

The kid didn't acknowledge his father. He put his hand out. Sal gave him time. He knew he was struggling. And his father right there breathing down his neck wasn't making it any easier. The next two pitches were high. Not close.

"Now let it come to you. You're in the driver's seat," his father said to him, trying to sound reasonable.

The next pitch was outside, but the kid swung and whiffed.

"What the hell? That was ball three! Even Osama would have called that one a ball. Use your brain!"

The kid ignored his father and backed away again. He stepped back into the box and got into his stance. He was visibly shaking. The pitcher went into the stretch and tested the outside corner again. The pitch was close—very close, but Sal kept his right hand down. Ball three—a full count now.

"You don't have to be the hero. You got help behind you," the loudmouth bellowed so all could hear. Every kid wants to be the hero, Sal thought. That's why they play the game. But numbnuts couldn't understand that.

The pitcher went into the stretch, let loose with the pitch. The batter started to flinch with his bat and then pulled it back. From where Sal was positioned, hunched over the catcher, the ball nicked the outside corner. He hesitated for just a moment and then his right arm went up. "Strike three," he said in an almost matter-of-fact way not wanting to show anyone up, especially a sixteen-year-old.

Within seconds, he heard the backstop shake behind him.

"Strike three? That pitch was two feet outside. You punch out my son? You got a problem with me, you take it up with me. Not my son. Bad call. Bad call, dammit!"

The man was pressed up against the backstop. Sal didn't respond. He started walking to get his water. The man was shadowing him through the backstop. "Don't play mute with me, Osama."

He could feel the spittle flowing from the man, showering him through the backstop. Sal took a breath, turned, and walked over to the coach of the kid's team. "Game is over unless someone removes that gentleman from the premises," he said calmly, but loud enough for the man to hear.

"You think I'm leaving. Get out from behind the backstop and we'll see what's what."

Staring down the coach, Sal waited. "It was a bad call, Sal," the coach said.

"Don't you start with me now," Sal said, raising his voice for the first time. "Don't make me toss you."

The coach shook his head and went to escort the loudmouth to the parking lot.

Sal could see the man push the coach's arm away when he tried to calm him. He looked back. "Go back to that prison where you belong," he screamed. Sal's work as a correction officer was public knowledge around the youth travel baseball leagues where he umpired and a reason most did not push him too hard on his calls. Still, there were those who didn't care. When it came to calls that went against your superstar son, all bets were off.

The game ended with a walk-off victory for the team the loudmouth's son played for. His so-called bad call had nothing to do with the outcome. If only these lunatic parents understood that.

He and his partner walked off the field as soon as the game ended, both heading to the parking lot where they would take off their pads and uniforms. His partner went down one end of the lot while Sal went to his truck. As he approached, the sun glinted off the shiny dark paint. But the glint was different. There was something else. Soon he was close enough to see the dent; a big gauge on the right rear fender. His first thought was that someone backed into him in the lot. But then he heard a snicker. "Ram tough, huh?"

Sal turned quickly. The blood was rushing to his head. He could take the verbal abuse. But this was something else. The loudmouth stood there, his bulging eyes on him. His arms were behind his back. Sal stared at him in disbelief. This was a line that had been crossed. "You did this?"

"I mean they say these trucks are built to take a beating. Looks like someone gave it one." He gave him that taunting grin.

Sal could see he was holding a bat behind him. He was egging him on. He wanted this. A kind of deep growl came from Sal's chest, but he said nothing.

"I guess someone swung and didn't miss."

People were now coming into the parking lot. Cameras were out. Sal's head was burning. It was like the sun was boiling his eyes and working back to his brain. His umpiring partner appeared. "File a complaint, Sal. I'll back you up. Let it go," his partner said, but Sal heard nothing.

"Come on, Osama. You think I'm gonna swing and miss? You think I don't know you made that call on my son because of me?"

The loudmouth brought the bat out in front of him. He stood his ground as Sal made his way to him.

He wasn't sure how long it lasted. Not long, that he knew. He could hear the cries behind him. The sobbing. He heard nothing else. His right hand ached and blood dripped from his knuckles. The loudmouth was flat on the pavement. The bat he hoped to use on Sal lay next to him. Blood that flowed from the loudmouth's head had gotten on the bat. Sal grabbed it. Looking at no one now, he took the bat, tossed it into the back seat, got into his truck and drove out of the parking lot.

By the time he got to the bar in Bayonne, he thought he had calmed. That his rage was spent. And it was—until that last Nestor comment by the dude with the greasy hair. So what if he called him Nestor, he reflected on now? They were just names. Was that justification for shattering a man's face? Of course not, but by the time he was done with him, there was blood all over the bar.

‡

The girl on the bed didn't need to know what he did just a few hours before they met. She sat with her head down and her hands clasped.

He got up and looked out the window. The black Challenger was still there. "What do they want? Those men in that car."

"Money," she said.

"They want you to get money from me? For this?" He gestured to the bed.

She nodded, her head down. "Until I pay them all for what they do for me." She started to pull up her yellow polo shirt. Sal shook his head at her. She stopped.

"What did they do for you?"

"They get me here. Across. Not them. But people they work for. They do this to others. The money is too much. I can't ever pay. But if I don't give them something, they maybe take my son. That's what they say."

"That's what they say?" Sal stared at her.

"They say five thousand, but it change all the time. It go up."

Sal nodded, got up, and went to the door. "Stay here. I'll be right back."

He had to go outside to get downstairs to the motel lobby. He glanced at the Challenger. It was still there. Through the tinted windows in the dark of night he could see some light inside, but nothing else. He went into the small motel lobby. "ATM?" he asked the clerk behind the desk. Sal seemed to startle the clerk. There was a fearful look on his face as if he was expecting trouble. He backed away from the desk and then pointed to an ATM behind the door.

Sal hesitated. He knew he had very little time. He took out his card and punched in his code. He had over three thousand in his checking account. He had more in a savings account with another bank. He had no use for money now. He tried to withdraw a thousand dollars, but the machine balked. He assumed there was a withdrawal limit, He tried eight hundred. Again, it spit his card out. He went down to six hundred and finally six, hundred dollar bills, whooshed out. He took the money, inserted his debit card and tried for another six hundred. He got a message that his daily withdrawal limit was reached. He had another hundred and fifty in his wallet. She could have it all.

He went back outside and up to the motel room. She was standing waiting for him. She had her cell phone in her hand. "I have to go. They see you leave the room." He took the phone from her and looked at it. There was a text in Spanish. He didn't need to ask what was on the text.

"What's your name?" He realized he never even bothered to ask her and neither did she.

"Zorry," she said.

"Zorry, take this." He held the seven hundred and fifty dollars he had.

She stared at it. "You give this to me."

"It's all I could get today."

"So much. I never get this much."

He didn't need to know anything else about her and what she had to do for them. "Go to them, but don't give them the money until you see me and I tell you to."

She looked confused.

"Just take the money, Zorry. When you see me, I will nod and you can give the money to them. Understand?"

She didn't answer but stuffed the money in her jeans and hurried to the door. He was right behind her. They went down to the parking lot. She walked toward the Challenger and stood a few feet from the car, waiting for his signal. Sal walked to his truck and opened the back door. The bat was on the seat. He grabbed it. As he started walking to the Challenger, he could hear sirens over the hum of the trucks and cars adjacent to the 222. He didn't have much time.

He moved around the truck with the bat in his hand. He heard voices speaking in Spanish, Zorry's and the men in the car. He gripped the bat tightly as he moved behind the Challenger. He wasted no time, swinging hard, smashing the bat into the red rear parking lights of the Challenger. He heard Zorry scream. "Back away," he yelled to her. "Go. Leave."

One man shot out of the driver's seat and turned to him. It was hard to make him out in the darkness. Sal took another swing putting another dent in the car's rear. Both men were out now. He couldn't see their faces, but he saw their guns. The sirens were getting louder. Colored lights from police cars were flashing over the parking lot. The two men turned to the flashing lights as they approached. Police cars were filling the lot.

The men shoved the guns into their pants and quickly got back into the Challenger. Sal ran to the driver's door. The dark window was up. Sal swung the bat. Glass shattered. Blood sprayed from the driver's neck. The Challenger took off, its tires screeching as it slammed into another car in the lot. The man who had been in the passenger's seat burst out of the car and started to run.

"Machado!" he heard someone behind him yell. He ignored the warning and started to run after the man fleeing the Challenger. Sal held the bat high as he ran.

"Drop the bat," the same voice yelled. He ignored it.

The man he was chasing ran, without looking, out onto the traffic on 222. There was a dull thump and the man flew up in the air before dropping hard to the street. Cars screeched trying to avoid running over the prone man.

"Now, Machado!"

Sal stopped. He was done. He dropped the bat. As he turned slowly, he saw that Zorry was gone. He was ready for this. He welcomed it now. He put his right hand in his pocket.

"Hands out and up!"

He kept his hand in his pocket. There was a row of cops with guns pointed in his direction.

"Hands out and up!" the policeman repeated.

Sal slowly pulled his right hand out of his pocket, mimicking as if he was pulling out a gun. He raised his right arm and pointed with his index finger. Sal was sure it wasn't a bad call. It nicked the outside corner. It was a strike. And then the air whooshed from his body.

Brian Silverman's work has been published in Mystery Tribune, Down and Out magazine, Mystery Magazine, Vautrin, and Rock and a Hard Place (January 2025). He has had stories included in *The Best American Mystery Stories 2018*, *The Best American Mystery and Suspense Stories 2021*, and one selected as a notable story in *The Best American Mystery Stories of 2019*. His 2021 novel, *Freedom Drop* will be reissued in 2025 along with its sequel, *Calypso Blue*.

VACATIONLAND

Gabriela Stiteler

It was early on Sunday morning at the end of the summer season and I was at Tony's picking up donuts and a copy of the *Quoddy Tides*. Tony had died three years earlier from the sort of wasting cancer that eats a person from the inside. Bill and Cindy, Tony's son and daughter-in-law, had taken the reins, Eastport being one of those small towns where businesses were passed down and kept running through a combination of masochistic generational guilt and stubborn, blue-collar work ethic.

Bill would sooner sell a piece of his soul than let the place sink.

"Morning Cindy," I said.

She was a thin, blonde woman who had spent her early years on her father's boat and her skin had weathered like a piece of driftwood.

She looked up at me and shoved the paper she was reading across the counter. "Did you hear about this?"

It was a flyer with a school picture of a smiling teenager with blonde hair and blue eyes. Jennifer Thomas. "Missing," it said

"Her parents own that summer place down past the old cannery," Cindy went on. "Usually she would have been at one of those sleepaway camps, but this year she's been with her family."

"Huh," I said. The girl in the picture looked young and fresh and a little wide-eyed.

"I seen her a few times by the water. Walking up and down the coast. You seen her with Scottie ever?"

Scottie was my grandson. He lived with his mom and stepdad in Portland but since the age of five, he'd spent summers with me. We got along fine. He and his stepfather did not. After Linda left me, for all the usual reasons, I'd been alone. Me and my cabin and the quiet. Scottie was the only real company I had due to the sort of life choices men sometimes make and, if we're lucky, survive g enough to regret. I didn't force conversation and neither did Scottie, who'd always been a bit an old soul. Comfortable with fishing and campfires and puzzles on the porch in the rain and Steve Earle records. Scottie was a little rough around the edges but a hard-working kid.

I couldn't picture him with that sweet, smiling girl.

"They're about the same age. Two kids from out of town," Cindy went on, almost cautiously.

I shook my head. "Not Scottie. Works hard at Carter's Lumberyard then comes back. Rinse and repeat, you know him. Kid keeps to himself."

Cindy had put my donuts, two molasses for me and two jelly powdered for Scottie, into a white paper bag, watching me all the while. "Maybe you want to ask him," she said. "Just to see. The girl's mom was in yesterday and she looked awful. Like she's aged about twenty years since the last time I saw her. Was saying her daughter's had a tough year. Seemed to think the cops weren't taking it seriously."

Cindy was a true Downeaster who both needed and resented vacationers. For her to care about a woman from away?

"It'll be okay. She'll turn up," I said, suddenly aware of how hot the bakery kitchen had become.

"Right," she said. "I'm sure it's nothing. But ask Scottie just in case, will you?" From the way she was gripping the bag and staring at me, I got the sense she was concerned. And her concern was catching. A feeling of discomfort lodged in my chest.

"I'll ask him," I said as I took the bag from her. "No harm in that. But I'm sure the girl just met up with some friends. Maybe even a boyfriend. Kids do that sort of thing, right?"

Cindy nodded. "Right. I'm sure that's what it is."

She turned her attention to the kitchen and I took my donuts and copy of the paper and made my way to my truck.

It was a beautiful summer day, the sort that belonged on a postcard to be sold to vacationers with the sun and the water and the seagulls and the statue of a fisherman wearing a yellow slicker. It was early enough where things still smelled faintly of salt. In a few hours, that would give way to the musky smell of the mud flats during a low tide.

As I drove home, I told myself that Jennifer Thomas was fine. That she'd turn up hungover and sheepish and sorry for having caused the concern. Kids made all sorts of bad choices.

Christ knew I had.

I hoped that, whatever the choice, it was something she could learn from. That she might laugh about it later with a husband or her own children. That it might be a story that began, "You wouldn't believe what I did when I was your age…"

‡

Scottie was off Sundays, because the Carter family, who owned and operated the lumberyard, was devout in a way that I admired but did not understand. His other free day was Thursday. We'd fallen into the habit of taking the boat out into the bay and out further still into the ocean and casting out lines. I'd bring a cooler with bait, usually shrimp, and green tea that was mostly sugar. We'd sit and listen to the water and drink the tea and sometimes catch a mackerel or herring or bluefish or something that we could grill and eat for dinner.

And so, on Wednesday I found myself at Moran's Market, filling the cooler with ice, getting gas for the boat, and enough shrimp to catch us something.

Jennifer Thomas's picture was plastered on the bulletin board. Still missing.

Moran's Market was a small, mom-and-pop type gas station with souvenirs and bait and ice. Inside, a tall, lean man who looked like he'd sprung from the pages of a LL Bean catalog was standing at the counter. When I got closer, I recognized him as Fred Thomas. Jessica's father. I'd only seen the guy around on a few occasions and he seemed harmless enough, well-intended and a little aloof.

The grief and helplessness radiating off the man was palpable and I kept my distance, pretending to look around for something on the shelves.

"You sure you didn't see anything?" He was asking Candy, the woman working the register who was blonde from a bottle and tan from a can with bright pink nails and a nicotine patch peeking out from under her uniform sleeves. Candy, who I knew from AA

and who I dutifully pretended not to know well.

She looked uncomfortable. "Look," she said, eyeing the door. "I already talked to the cops. Didn't see anything. Hear anything. I swear."

The man's shoulders slumped inward and I wondered how many other places he'd gone, how many other people he'd asked the same question to.

"I'm sorry," Candy said in a lower voice. "Really. I wish I could help. I'm sure she'll turn up. Okay?"

"Sure," he said. "Right."

But his voice was flat and the way he stood for another minute, blinking at her and not moving, I wondered if he was on the edge of breaking down.

"I have other customers," she said, not unkindly.

"Of course," he said. "I'm sorry."

And then he left.

I waited until the door closed before I approached the counter.

Candy was staring at the flyer he'd left.

I cleared my throat and put the green tea down.

She forced a smile. "Hi ya, Sam," she said.

I nodded.

"The usual?"

I nodded again and she rang me up.

"Damned shame about that girl, isn't it? The sort of thing you read about but you never think will happen where you live," she went on. "What I mean is there's no way that girl is still alright. I seen her before, walking around with those mini bottles of Fireball, smiling at the wrong sorts of men. Trouble, that's for sure. Loud. And looking a hell of a lot older than sixteen."

I shifted on my feet, not much wanting to hear anything bad

about the kid who'd gone missing, preferring to think of her as the smiling, wide-eyed girl on the flyer.

Candy, however, was not done. "That kind of girl never goes radio silent unless something bad has happened. Takes one know one. That'll be forty-two dollars and some change."

I gave her forty-three.

"You really talk to the cops?" I asked.

She nodded and counted out my change. "Think they're making the rounds and talking to everyone. Surprised they haven't made it out to you, yet. Told them what I knew. Which wasn't much. But it doesn't make sense to tell her father that, does it? What good would it do to tell that man that his baby was looking for all sorts of trouble and that everyone in town knew it? Seems better to let it be, don't you think?"

"Sure. Maybe." I dropped the change into the tin, said my goodbyes, and backtracked to the door before grabbing the ice and bait.

Next to the ice locker, in a green Subaru with a rack on top, Fred Thomas sat, staring forward, clutching the wheel.

I pretended not to see him, got into my truck, closed the door, and drove away.

✝

My place was at the end of a gravel road off the main drag. A wood frame cabin with one bedroom, a woodstove, and well water that always smelled a little like sulfur. The cabin itself was nothing special, but the little piece of land on which it sat? It was my own small slice of something worthwhile. I had a handful of acres with ocean access and a splintered dock for my boat, a 1931 Sparkman & Stephens Manhasset Bay One Design, which had come with the place.

Scottie's car was still gone, which meant he hadn't returned

from work. It was too early for dinner but too late to take on any of
the bigger projects I'd been scheming up. The biggest project,
which was half done, was the fence I'd started earlier that year
after the ground had thawed. I had the posts sunk, but I needed
Scottie's help with the panels. Most projects I could manage on my
own, but I couldn't do the panels without a second set of hands.
For me, Scottie was it. A right hand when I needed it.

The other project I'd been cooking up was to do with the old
playhouse Scottie and I had built when he was little. We framed
the thing up and outfitted it to be a place just for him. At that time,
things for him and his mom were tight and they were sharing a
one-bedroom apartment. Connor, my son and Scottie's father, was
already long gone by that point, having done lasting damage to
both his woman and his child.

Not that I was one to stand in judgment.

The damage done to Connor was more than half my fault,
after all.

Christ knew I'd made enough mistakes of my own.

Over the years, Scottie's playhouse had fallen on hard times
and I had been cooking up all sorts of ideas. Maybe Scottie would
like to come out and stay after he finishes school. Maybe I could
build one of those tiny homes for him.

Just in case.

Give him a place to land.

A future beyond the mess waiting for him in Portland.

The playhouse was behind a copse of river birches and red
twig dogwood that had grown unruly over the years. One of the
windows was broken and had been replaced with a piece of
plywood. The bottom planks were sagging, half-rotted, and slowly
being absorbed into the ground.

I pushed open the door tentatively. Inside, it smelled like a damp cigarette and cheap beer. In the corner, there was a sleeping bag, surrounded by empty Pabst cans, and a coffee tin filled with cigarette butts, some of which were covered with lipstick. And next to the sleeping bag, I spotted one of those empty Fireball bottles and a few silver condom wrappers. Scottie, it seemed, had found another use for his playhouse.

Half of me was proud of the kid who'd been too awkward to talk to anyone, let alone a girl, three years ago. But a few inches in height and some muscle and working in the sun had done something for his confidence. Christ, I'd been there myself once, a veritable lifetime ago. Only I hadn't thought about the condoms.

I made my way back up to the cabin, having decided to give Scottie one more summer with the playhouse. One more summer as a kid.

The shit hand he'd been dealt? He deserved that much.

I was halfway back when I caught the sound of gravel popping. A police cruiser wound down the driveway.

I leaned against one of those lonely fence posts and waited, feeling a little hot under my collar.

The cruiser ground to a stop and an officer emerged, looking young as hell.

I didn't recognize him, but then, there were lots of people I didn't know.

"You Sam?" He asked.

I nodded.

He handed me one of the flyers. Jennifer's face peered up at me.

"You hear about the missing girl?"

I nodded again. "Hard not to in a town small as this."

"You hear anything about her? See anything suspicious? Kids

from out of town or anything?"

I shrugged. "It's the summer. I've seen all sorts of people from away. Haven't heard much about the girl. Just that she's missing and her parents are worried sick."

The officer nodded. "That's the truth." He glanced behind me, at the cabin. "I heard your grandson is in town. He around?"

"No, sir," I said. "But he should be back soon. Working double time at Carter's this year."

The officer grinned and rocked back on his heels. "No shit. That was my summer job."

"It's good, hard work," I said.

"Yes, sir," he said and glanced at his watch. "That shift's done now. What time you expect him back?"

"Soon. Any minute really. You want me to grab you a green tea and you can wait on him?"

The officer glanced at the cruiser, shifted on his feet, glanced at the porch, and said, "I really shouldn't…"

From the way he said it, I figured it was what he was supposed to say. I also figured he wanted to drink the damned tea. I made for the cooler on the porch and he followed.

"You live around here?" I asked after I handed one to him.

He opened it, took a long sip, and then carefully screwed the lid back on. "Not anymore," he said. "But my grandpa did and I'd come up over the summers."

"No shit," I said, giving myself a breath to imagine Scottie in a few years with a future beyond the trouble he kept getting caught up with in Portland. "He still live around here?"

The officer's jaw tightened and he swallowed. "Passed away about five years back. Man smoked like a damned chimney."

"I'm sorry," I said. And I meant it.

"Not a day goes by that I don't think of him."

The way he said it, all serious and sad, I believed him. And I wanted, very badly, to be missed like that by someone. Above us, the sky was black and the tops of the trees had begun to sway the way they did before a storm rolled in.

Both of us were eyeing the sky as Scottie's car turned down the driveway.

"That him?" The officer asked.

I nodded.

Scottie got out, his yellow uniform t-shirt covered in sawdust and his cheeks and the bridge of his nose red from being in the sun. He was looking hot and tired and a little annoyed. He glanced at the cop, then at me.

"Officer," he said carefully.

I handed him the flyer. "Don't know if you seen this or heard about it, but a girl's gone missing. Family's sick looking for her."

Scottie stared at my hand but wouldn't take the flyer.

"Officer is here to see if we've heard anything," I went on.

Scottie looked back to the officer, who was watching the exchange, waiting.

"I heard about it at Carter's," Scottie began. "Everyone's talking about it. I saw her a few times, I think. But she didn't look like she does in this picture."

The cop nodded. "Hearing a lot of that."

"Don't know much about her, though. I'm not really from here. I just come up for the summer."

Again the cop nodded. "She wasn't from here either. Not really."

There was a pause after that. None of us seemed to know what to say.

Scottie cleared his throat. "Is there anything I can do to help?"

The cop reached into his pocket and removed some cards. He handed one to Scottie and one to me. "That's nice of you to ask. The biggest help for now is just to call if anything comes up. If you remember anything or notice anything that might shed some light on Jennifer's disappearance."

"Yes, sir," Scottie said.

And something in me loosened. There had been a time when Scottie was so angry he couldn't seem to help himself and I thought he'd end up in jail, like his father. Maybe things were getting better, easier for him. Maybe all it took was time. That's what I was thinking as he and I stood next to each other and watched the cop and his cruiser pull out of the driveway.

Scottie went inside to shower.

I started the grill and sat in one of the lawn chairs on the porch, and let myself think about a world in which he had a fighting chance at a future that wasn't shit.

He came out and we sat on the porch together, playing cards, and watching the rain.

Maybe, I thought, just maybe, the summers with me had been enough.

✢

I was nineteen when Connor was born.

His mom had told me about it during a fight. As a way to piss me off, it seemed at the time.

"You want to keep it?" I'd said, self-righteous anger burning through me. "Fine. But don't expect shit from me." I was a little drunk and a little angry and a lot scared and stupid. So very stupid. But, in that moment, it was exactly what I wanted to say.

When I was a few years older and wiser, I regretted it. The

words. My absence. Everything. But the damage had been done. There are some things a person can't come back from.

Scottie, who almost didn't make it to this world alive, whose mother tried her best but who had terrible taste in men, was a chance at redemption.

‡

The next morning, I had the cooler in the boat and had enough gas in the motor to get us out in the open water. I'd grabbed a thermos of coffee, enough for both of us. When Scottie was a kid, I'd bring juice boxes for him. That was back when I was still drinking and I'm ashamed to admit that at that time I would forgo coffee for a morning beer.

As we pulled away from the dock into the bay, I noticed a nylon line off the starboard side that was dragging. I opened my mouth to say something, but with the motor and the wind, I didn't quite get the words out. We were far enough away from the rocky coast, to that place where the ocean is vaster than the land and we, as people, are insignificant, ripples against waves.

I watched as Scottie took the hunting knife I'd given him for his thirteenth birthday from his pocket and reached out. I watched as he cut the line. I watched the line, weighed down by something heavy, disappear into the ocean.

We went further out, to the edge of what was safe.

And we cast out our lines.

Gabriela Stiteler is a writer based in Maine by way of the Rust Belt. Her debut short story, "Two Hours West of Nothing" (EQMM, 2023), was nominated for the MWA Fish Award and selected to be read on the podcast Rabia Chaudry Presents The Mystery Hour with AHMM and EQMM. Her second story was published in *The Best of New England Crime Writing (2023)*. Since then, she has had stories accepted to AHMM, EQMM, *The Best of New England Crimewriting* (2024), and *Shotgun Honey Presents: At the Edge of Darkness* (2024).

AVOIDING THE HOLES

Stanton McCaffery

Sitting on my nightstand, there's a game I've had since I was a kid. It's a wooden box with a maze on the top. You have to turn the box so a silver marble travels along the maze all the way to the end. There are holes every so often that you have to get the marble around, or else it falls into the box. The game's called Labyrinth. I still play it before I go to sleep.

There are books in my bedroom I've had since I was a kid too. Mythology, mostly. Greek, Roman, Norse. Monsters and heroes, Gods and fate. Tragedies. It's all relevant as a philosophy major. On top of my bookshelf is a sculpture of the Minotaur my parents got for me when I was eight. It scared the hell out of me when I unwrapped it, and at first, I could hardly look at it. Its horns were sharp to the touch. I kept it in my room but had to have a nightlight plugged in until I convinced myself it wasn't real, that all that stuff was made up.

When I played Labyrinth, I would pretend that when the marble fell into a hole it was eaten by the Minotaur.

I see people die sometimes and I feel like I'm watching them fall into a hole, like the marble, and they're going to be eaten by the Minotaur.

My walls are covered in art. My favorite is just a blue canvas with a human eye in the middle. They say eyes are the gateway to the soul. Some people believe your eyes contain your soul. When I've got someone who I know is going to die, I look at their eyes and I think about that.

My partner Ray doesn't think about much when he's in the back, and I'm driving and he's got somebody going down the tubes. "We ready to go?" he asks me in between drags on a cigarette.

It's 5AM and we're outside the office. Ray drives in the mornings, I do the supplies check, and we switch in the afternoon.

That's the deal we've got worked out. We get the job done together fine, as different as we are.

Most of the morning passes. A few routine calls. Difficulty breathing, a fender bender, a slip and fall. For our post, we don't have a building we're stationed at, just a rough area we need to stay in, so when the calls stop coming Ray drives to a park and gets out to smoke. I put my legs on the dashboard and read. Ray stands with the driver's side door open, one hand holding his cigarette and the other holding him up against the door. His gut is protruding to the point where I think the buttons on his shirt will burst.

"You're always thinking," he says and I nod. "That shit's not good for you."

Our alarm tone starts to blurt out on the radio. It's a five-second series of high-pitched beeps. Ray stamps out his cigarette, and I grab the clipboard and a run sheet to jot down the location.

"Metro 76," says the dispatcher, "respond to Demott and Harrison for the motor vehicle accident, one car, entrapment, unknown injuries."

Ray drives like Ray always drives: fast. The windows are open, and all I hear is some mixture of the siren and the wind, melded into one. We get on scene and there's a crowd of people surrounding a black SUV. A few police cruisers are already there. Fire is pulling up next to us, their lights are blinding. I hop out of the truck and approach, and Ray goes back to get the stretcher. Two officers are holding a woman, walking her back from the vehicle. She's screaming something incoherent. Her black hair is in her face and she's swinging her head back and forth. She kicks both feet in the air and the cops sit her down on the side of the street, still holding onto her.

I look around the pavement for a leak, a ruptured gas line.

We're good. Closer, I see a fence pole going into the front of the SUV and coming out of the back. I come to the side and I'm stuck, my legs are blocks of ice. I drop the clipboard.

For my first two years on the job, I was lucky: no bad pediatric calls.

Everyone's luck runs out eventually.

There's a girl in the passenger seat, ten, tops, and the fence pole is through her right eye. The end at the other side of her head has blood on it and something else, something white. I hear Ray behind me, "You gotta get inside, kid."

A fireman breaks a back window and puts cloth over the door. I cram myself into the back seat. There are shards of glass with the sun reflecting off them that I'm careful not to put my hand in. My eyes hurt from the bouncing light. Sometimes it's better not to look directly at things.

I know that Fire is trying to get the front passenger side door open but I can't hear them over the mother's screams. "Hi sweetheart," I say to the girl. "Can you hear me? Can you tell me your name?"

"Kate," she says. Her voice is flat, like she's having a regular day-to-day conversation, like I'm fitting her for a pair of sneakers. Jesus.

"Keep that airway clear," I hear Ray say from the outside. He starts handing me gauze through the window. He can't stop staring at the girl's face.

"Okay, Kate," I say. "My name is David. I'm going to stay here with you."

"Can you hold my hand?" she says.

It's unbelievably soft, and it's cold and sweaty. She's got painted fingernails, black with tiny stars. They get the door open and cut as much of the pole as possible. Ray helps me configure her on the stretcher as I hold an oxygen mask onto what's left of her face.

A block away from the hospital she stops talking. I let her hand go to start chest compressions. I look at her eye. Ray's taking potholes a hundred miles an hour and my feet are coming a foot off the floor of the ambulance. Her eye is green with little sparkles of brown.

We rush through the winding halls of the ER. When we get her to the code room an army of nurses lifts her onto a bed. Ray transfers our tubes to their oxygen tanks and gives a report. I look at her hand dangling off the bed.

They close a hospital curtain around me, and I hear a doctor inside, "Time of death 11:47 AM." Ray walks past me with the stretcher on his way back to the ambulance.

That night I'm in my bed, trying to get the marble to the end of the Labyrinth and angels appear outside my bedroom window, under a streetlight. At least I think they're angels; they've got wings. There are two of them and they're trying to get my attention, waving and speaking, but I can't hear them. I sit up but they fly away, laughing, like they're teasing me. I spend the night getting only fits and spurts of sleep. I look at my bookshelf and I wonder if anything in any of those books could explain what I experienced earlier in the day. The light from the outside casts a shadow on everything. It never bothered me before but now it's unsettling, like I'm aware of something.

Early in the morning, with little quality sleep, I'm dreading the day ahead. Another 13 hours with Ray, talking about nothing and carting around the nearly dead.

The angels come back.

I can't see them too well. I go outside and, standing under the light, it's clear they're not what I thought.

With their little clawed hands, they're throwing something small and round and mostly white. They're catching it perfectly despite their lack of eyes. They've got little red tails and black wings.

"This is what we take," they say in unison. "You're better off without."

My legs are frozen again. My childhood church used to have a mural of angels in the clouds. I used to think they were dancing and that, when I died, I would go and dance with them. I run back inside and throw up in the bathroom. The mirror shows me a face I don't recognize, gaunt and lifeless.

When I get to the office, I'm unable to talk. Ray takes it for tiredness.

"Get this shit," he says after we've packed the ambulance and we're on our way to our post, "a buddy of mine that works at Saint Pete's says someone messed with that girl's body. He says they went to get her ready to give her over to the funeral home and found her other eye was missing."

Ray says someone.

Someone.

Birds are chirping outside, and I watch them as they chase each other on the tree branches without a care.

In the game of Labyrinth, it's easy to fall into a hole and get lost, especially if you think too much.

Just move through it. That's what my dad used to say when I would get frustrated with it. You shouldn't even look at it too much, he would say.

Ray moves his sizeable mass out from behind the steering wheel and smokes outside with the door open, on autopilot, like always. He coughs his smoker's cough and it pierces my ears and makes me wince but it doesn't seem to cause Ray any pain at all.

"I can still feel her hand," I say to him. Her eye is what's on my mind at the moment, but I don't say anything about that.

He coughs again. "Put it out of your mind, kid." Keeping focus on me, he crushes one cigarette with his foot and lights another.

My hands are shaking and he's looking but he doesn't say anything about them. "And for Christ's sake, don't go anywhere to talk to a professional about it."

Ray comes back inside the ambulance, and we spend the rest of the day sitting in the park without a call. The sun beats down on me through the windshield. He gets out and smokes a bunch more, but we go the rest of the hours without saying much. Like I'm scratching at a scab and turning it into an open wound, I think the whole time about going and telling someone about how I feel, about what I've seen, about what went on outside my window under the streetlight.

I can't sleep again at night, and it's worse this time because that's all I want to do, to close my eyes and forget everything. My mind is reeling. Like a wheel broken free mid-journey from a bicycle, it goes where it wants. It flashes images. Nothing in the order it occurred, just snapshots of sight and sound. Screaming. The mother's shaking head and black hair. The girl's hand. The calm of her voice. Did she suffer?

Of course she did.

The Minotaur on my bookshelf is looking at me. He's got his head tilted downward so his horns point towards my face. I take him down and throw him in the garbage.

"This isn't a game anymore," I say.

Outside, in the street, under the light, they're back. They're tossing the little white thing again. I pick up the Labyrinth game and run outside. Under the light I feel naked, exposed. They see me coming and they float down to eye level. Closer than I've been before I can make out their grotesque nature, raw oozing skin and eyeless faces with long beak-like noses. I throw the wooden box at them and they dodge it. It shatters in the street, shards of wood fly at my legs. The marble makes a pinging sound as it rolls into the gutter.

"Why are you here?" I yell.

They laugh. It's high-pitched and broken, like they've sucked on helium and gargled glass. One of them holds out the white ball in his small hand. In front of me, I can see it has red veins and a patch of color on one side, green and some brown. I knew what it was the last time they came, but I didn't want to think about it. I knew as soon as Ray told me what happened to the girl's body.

"Give us yours and you won't see us anymore," they say, together. They sing it in mock children's voices, like they're following the bouncing ball on a cartoon. I turn and run and I can hear them behind me. "Give us yours. Give us yours. Then we'll give it to him." A block away and I keep going. Ray wouldn't approve of where I'm heading. There's only one other choice as I see it: go back to my apartment and tie one end of an extension cord around my neck and the other end around a leg of my bed and then jump out of the window. Not much of a choice, I know, so I keep running.

On my way, I think, once I arrive, they'll do something to make me better. At the very least they'll talk to me, tell me something that will calm me down. I step through the ER's automatic doors and I know I'm wrong.

"There is no end," the nurse says to me when she takes my name.

Sitting next to me is a woman with her face covered by a

black veil.

She leans over, her shoulder bumping into mine.

"I've seen him too," she says. I turn and look at her and she lifts the veil. It's the girl's mother. Her face has rotted, pasty translucent skin, spotted green and purple. Her lips are raw and bloody. She speaks again and I see broken black and yellow teeth, worms on her tongue. "The bull man," she says. "And his friends too."

I get up, terrified, and walk to the other side of the ER. "Nurse," I say, "can I please be seen soon?" My nerves are a knotted mess and my heart's hammering.

She walks to me with her clipboard and gives me a stern look. "There is no end."

There's a woman with two children playing with a toy at her feet. No clue what kind of toy it is but they're fighting over it, pushing each other back and forth. They're singing something that at first I can't decipher, but when I step closer I make out the words. It's the same bouncing-ball cartoon song I heard only minutes earlier. "Give us yours and you won't see us anymore."

Before I can scream, the nurse comes over. "He will see you now." She walks through a set of double doors and I follow her. She points at a section of hallway partitioned by a hanging curtain. "He is waiting for you." Up, poking out from the top of the curtains is a pair of horns.

Again, I turn and run. There are heavy footsteps behind me. In the waiting room, the nurse is holding a bent fence pole. The children are still singing. "Give us yours and you won't see us anymore." They throw their toy at me and it clings to my shoulder. I'm out the door when I look at it. It's her hand. I can tell by the nail polish, black with tiny stars. When I pull it off and throw it in the street, it feels the same, cold and incredibly soft.

This is it. My only other option is in a toolbox under my bed.

When I get back to my apartment, the door is open a crack, but I don't care because I figure I left it that way. In my bedroom, he's there, sitting on my bed with his enormous arms crossed. His horns are scratching the ceiling. He's holding one end of the extension cord and the other end is tied around the bed post.

"You've fallen in the hole, I'm afraid," he says. "But there is another option."

‡

When Ray comes by to bring me pizza two months later, I don't see him staring at the deep grooves the horns dug into my ceiling, but I know he is. I figure it's a safe bet he's looking up at them whenever he isn't staring at me and the bandages covering my empty eye-holes.

I hear him put his hand on my bookshelf. He bumps into the painting of the eye that's hanging next to it and spends a minute fidgeting with it.

"So, kid," he says, "what are you gonna do with these books now that you can't read them?"

"Throw them out," I say. "Throw them out."

Stanton McCaffery is the Editor-in-Chief at Rock and a Hard Place Press. His short stories have been featured in Mystery Tribune, Mystery Weekly, Guilty, Vautrin, and Shotgun Honey. He has published two novels: *Into the Ocean*; and *Neighborhood of Dead Ends*. His short story, "Will I See The Birds When I Am Gone," which was originally published in Dark Yonder, will be featured in *Best American Mystery and Suspense 2024*. His third novel is currently on submission.

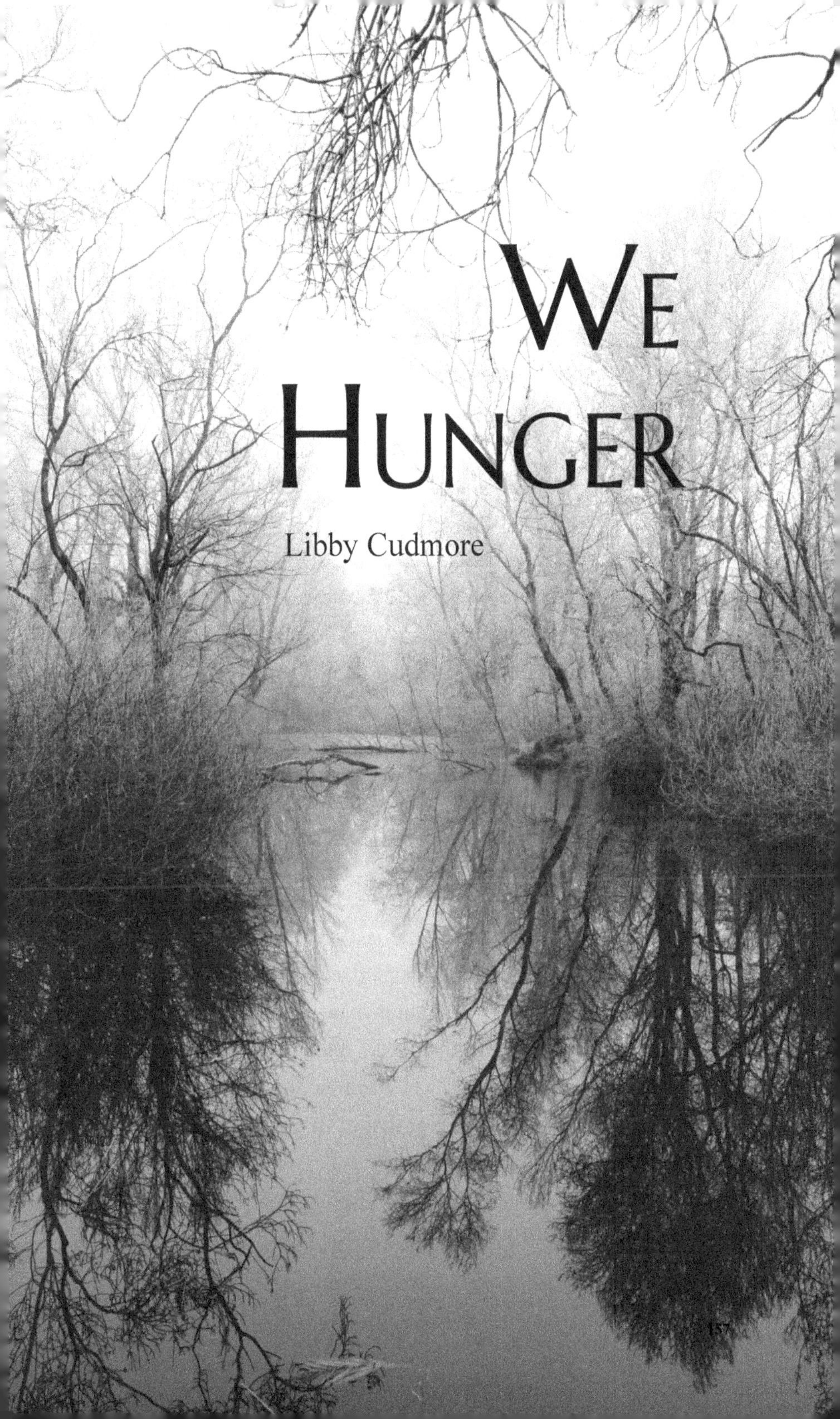

WE
HUNGER
Libby Cudmore

It started with water running down Main Street. A trickle overnight, but within two days it was a small stream to be stepped over. Children raced leaves and paper boats. No one in Truce was fully aware of the source; the mayor told everyone not to worry. Minor flooding from spring thaw. It will dry up in a week. But two weeks later, Mouse observed, the water seemed wider and deeper than before

‡

"Did you hear about the Cassidys?" Rope asked, leaning against the back wall of the Taco Bell. "Ate their kid. Three months old. Just…ate him."

Of course Mouse had heard. The Cassidys lived two doors down from her parents. She heard the sirens, the anguished wails. She saw the sheriff's deputies lead them out of the house, faces hidden in pillowcases. She imagined this was so that no one would see the blood on their mouths. Her stepmother, Stephanie, had caught her staring out the window and yanked the blinds down angrily. Show some respect, she'd snapped. Let them have their space.

Poor Laurie. She'd babysat him a few times while Denise went to the doctor or to get a haircut. He was a sweet baby, quiet and happy. The Cassidys were the last people anyone would suspect of this crime. The Morgans, that made sense. The Morgans were monsters. When they ate their three-year-old, Meegan, everyone just blamed it on their meth habit. But Denise and Robert Cassidy had no such excuse. At least none that anyone knew of.

Watch came out with the garbage. "It's in the water," he said. "Brain-eating amoebas."

"Where'd you read that?" She snorted. "The National Orbit?"

"Yeah man," he said. "Support local journalism."

"Support your local crackpot," Rope said.

"You laugh," he said. "But no one ate their babies before the water came."

He had a point.

‡

Mouse climbed in her bedroom window. She was late and she knew it. She could deal with the consequences in the morning. "Mouse?" she heard in a small voice.

Tonya was waiting on her bed, holding the oversized Rainbow Brite doll that used to be Mouse's. Her half-sister had been a surprise, according to Stephanie, but Mouse didn't entirely believe that. A baby is a good way to hold onto a husband, especially a baby born just two years after Mouse's mom died. Mouse couldn't blame her dad, and she didn't mind Tonya most of the time, especially now that she'd outgrown her habit of unwinding all her tapes.

"You should be in bed," she said.

"I am in bed," Tonya replied.

"You should be in your bed."

Tonya shook her head. "I want to sleep in here," she insisted. "I'm scared."

"Scared of what?"

"That Mommy and Daddy will eat me."

She sat next to her sister. She put her arm around her, breathing in her sticky-sweet Barbie shampoo scent. "No one will hurt you," she said. "Not while I'm around."

"You promise?"

She pulled back the covers. She tucked Tonya into her bed. "I promise," she said. "Go to sleep. I'll be in soon."

Mouse put on her pajamas. She brushed her teeth and scrubbed her face and put her hair in braids. Her stomach grumbled; the tacos Rope brought her hadn't been enough to satiate her. For a moment, she feared The Hunger had taken her. But the feeling passed as quickly as it came on. She went down to the kitchen and pulled a knife from the butcher block by the stove. She slipped it inside her pillowcase and hoped she never had to use it.

⁜

Their Senator, John McCormick, relayed that the Travis Dam was working as intended. Someone asked him about the rash of baby eating, and all he said was that he was praying for everyone involved. Letters to the editor and talking heads on TV news blamed absent fathers, drugs from Mexico, the lack of prayer in schools. On Saturday, the sheriff's deputies arrested another man who ate his toddler daughter while her mother was at work. No one would answer any questions about where the water was coming from.

⁜

Same as it ever was, Mouse thought as she applied eyeliner. Rope was so good at making mix tapes. Songs for the Flood might have his strongest creation yet; "Once in a Lifetime," "The Killing Jar," "Jump in the River." She'd found it in her mailbox that morning. He must have dropped it off after his shift.

Over the Doobie Brothers "Black Water" she heard Tonya shriek from downstairs. "Daddy, no!" she screamed. "Daddy, stop!"

"Bill, stop!" Stephanie said. "Bill, get away from her!"

She dropped her eyeliner. She took the stairs two at a time just as Stephanie made her way into the foyer and shoved Tonya into her arms. "Get her out of here," Stephanie said. "Get my pocketbook and take the car."

"What about you?"

Her father rounded the corner out of the kitchen. His eyes were bloodshot, his mouth twisted and agape. "Go!" Stephanie said, grabbing an umbrella and swinging it like a sword. "Get out of here!"

Tonya's shrieks in her ears were deafening. For a second, she wondered if she was immune; so far, the parents with The Hunger only ate small children. But was it size or bloodline that drove them to such horror? If he caught them, would her father spare her, or devour her too?

She made it to the car. Stephanie drove a red Corvette, like the Barbie car she bought Tonya for her birthday. There wasn't time to get the car seat out of her father's station wagon. She didn't know where she was going to go, only that she had to get out of there. She could still hear Stephanie screaming at her dad. Hold him off just a few minutes longer, she begged silently. She just had to hope that The Hunger wasn't contagious.

Water pooled around her ankles. The stream was no longer contained to the street. It was filling their yard faster than she could comprehend. Had the Truce dam broken? Was this the Biblical flood? Was she dreaming all of it?

She pulled Tonya from the back seat as the water reached her knees. "What's happening?" she shrieked.

Mouse didn't have an answer. "Doggy paddle!" was all that came out. "Like Mommy and Me class. Try and stay above water."

"But Mommy isn't here!"

The water was up to her chest. Drowned bodies, dogs, and neighbors, floated by. She saw her street sign, Adcox Way, pulled from the cement by the force of the flood. She considered letting the deep take them. She had nothing left to keep her afloat. Her arms, her legs, her whole being was exhausted from trying to hold up Tonya and fight the water that threatened to drag them down.

A buoy floated by, from the pool at the playground down the street. "Hold onto this," she said, wrapping the rope loosely around her sister's tiny wrist. "Don't let go, okay?"

It was advice she couldn't take herself. A deluge threw her off the buoy, pulling her from Tonya. She tried to swim against the current, but it was filling Truce like a teacup, a basin, a bathtub. The waves pushed them further and further apart, until she couldn't hear her sister's cries anymore.

‡

Hey. I know this one.

Is she alive?

Heavenly Father, please let this girl live. In Jesus' name, we pray.

Mouse opened her eyes. She was staring sideways at trees. Her clothes were wet, but she was on dry land. Rope was crouched next to her. Watch was there with him, and another boy she didn't recognize. She sat up and tried to speak, but all that came out of her mouth was water. "Where?" she managed to sputter. "Where is Tonya?"

"No idea," he said. "We haven't found her yet."

She wobbled to her feet. She was still drenched, her braids half-undone. "I have to get home," she insisted. "I have to find Tonya. I have to find Stephanie. My dad…my dad had The Hunger. I need to know they're okay."

"There's no home, Mouse," Rope said. "The town is underwater."

This had to be a nightmare. Had to be a movie she was acting out in her head. Her whole body felt as though she'd been riding roller coasters all day; her bones were cold jelly, her skin hot paper. "What about your parents?" she asked.

He shook his head. "The park got hit hard," he said. "The

water just…just demolished the trailers. No one could have survived that. I washed up about a mile from here. A couple of other kids did too. This guy, Declan, came in from Delhi, said he was going to take us to a safe house. Says he's Senator McCormick's brother. See if he can't reunite us with other family members."

She fell into his arms. She murmured I'm sorry. She tried to imagine Tonya still clinging to her buoy, washing up safely downstream the same way Mouse had. Maybe she had dreamed her father's hunger as she drifted downstream. How could she mourn the man who wanted to devour her?

The papers predicted this, Watch said. He introduced the other kid as Preach. Preach got in a canoe he built when the water started to rise, but his parents had both been at a church meeting. It was unknown if they had survived.

✝

Declan had a checkered shirt, dark jeans, hiking boots, and a brown flight jacket he draped over Mouse when he saw her shivering. There was another girl with him, cradling a newborn. He introduced her as Miranda. She introduced the baby as Charlie. His father had drowned trying to get them to safety.

"Did you find anyone else?" Declan asked.

"Only the bodies of sinners," Preach said. "The ones God refused to spare when he cleansed the Earth."

"Shut up, Preach," Watch sneered. "Your parents drowned too."

✝

Declan had a Chevy pickup with a blue stripe. Mouse and Miranda got to ride inside for what felt like hours, or maybe only minutes between long, tired blinks. Every time she woke up, she hoped she had dreamed it all. Every time she snapped awake, she

was still in the truck of a man she'd known for all of 20 minutes, hoping that he really was the Senator's brother and not the kind of monster their mothers all warned them about.

Senator John McCormick was waiting with a wide smile and a stack of pizza boxes at the biggest house she'd ever seen.

"Welcome," he said. "I'm so sorry for what you've been through, and please know that whatever you need, we're going to try and provide until you can be reunited with your families."

"How did this happen?" Mouse heard herself saying aloud. "How come we weren't warned?"

Preach shushed her quietly. Shut up, Rope whispered. Senator McCormick stepped forward and put his hands on her shoulders. His fingers pulled the warmth from her body. He looked into her eyes. "We're working on figuring that out," he said gently. "But I promise you, we'll get to the bottom of it."

He released her. He promised there was other food if and when they wanted it. There were private chefs in shiny kitchens, ready to feed them until they burst. There would be new clothes from catalogs piled on the sideboard. A Nintendo in the game room. In the morning, there would be a press conference to try and reunite them with their families.

"What if our families didn't survive?" Rope asked.

Senator McCormick smiled sadly. He put his hand on Rope's shoulder. "Then you can stay here as long as you like."

‡

The papers carried their photos. The news interviewed them. There were other stories of reunification on the news every evening. Kids from their school. Families from Mouse's neighborhood. No one mentioned The Hunger. No one said where the floods came from. And no one came for Rope, Watch, Preach, Miranda, or Mouse.

Days fell off the calendar like Tetris blocks. Senator McCormick went to the Capital for work, promised he'd be back in a few days, promised he'd keep looking, promised to allocate funds for the survivors to rebuild their lives. If they needed anything, the house was theirs.

"We should throw a rager," Watch joked.

"There's no one to invite," Rope said.

At night, Mouse dreamed of Tonya. Dreamed of the flood. Dreamed of The Hunger. Dreamed that she was floating on the gentle waves of the kiddie pool when a great white shark rose up from the cement depths. In these dreams, she knew her father and Stephanie were dead. There was no one to save Tonya but her.

Her sister's screams didn't stop when she woke up drenched in her own salt-water sweat. The screams weren't coming from inside her head.

They were coming from Miranda's room

The worst part wasn't the screams. The worst part was the silence. Declan tried her door. Locked. "Miranda," he pleaded. "Miranda, please, open the door."

Mouse's legs felt like ice pops. She already knew what they'd find. She didn't want to see the blood, the torn limbs, the anguish. At least it had been quick, she tried to tell herself.

Declan kicked open the door. The scent of wet copper filled Mouse's nostrils. Miranda lay slumped against the bassinet. It was hard to tell where all the blood was coming from, as though she might drown in it, flooding her mouth, slick on her hands, dripping in snakes down her wrists. The dried smears on the white bassinet told them there would be nothing to save inside.

Declan gathered Miranda into his arms, fumbling his fingers

around her throat to find her pulse. Her eyes fluttered open. "I'm sorry," she whispered. "I…I couldn't…I couldn't fight it."

Mouse crouched next to her, murmuring safe affirmations they both knew were lies. She wanted to ask what flesh tasted like. If it was as succulent as the first watermelon of summer, or if it tasted like chicken, boiled and bland. Was it worth it? Did it fulfill the craving, or was the disappointment the first piece of the horror and guilt that emerged?

She kicked a kitchen knife underneath the bed. She helped Declan bandage Miranda's wrists with strips Rope tore from t-shirts. Preach and Watch were waiting outside as the medics carried her away. They could hear her anguish from the bottom of the stairs.

In the bassinet, Charlie lay still and red, his neck broken, a few bites taken from his chest. Declan wrapped him in a blanket. "We'll clean him up," he murmured. "And when she's ready, we'll bury him."

‡

Mouse gathered up wildflowers as best she could, snuck in a few roses from the front bushes while the gardener was on a smoke break, and made her way to the medical ward at the back of the house. It was a paltry offering, but it was all she had. No one had heard from Miranda since they took her to the back of the house. Mouse was worried about her.

The room was white, sterile, and as empty as a swimming pool in January. There was no sign Miranda had even been there. Had she died and no one told them? They were holding Charlie in the chest freezer until he could be buried, but if he could be buried alongside his mother, she wanted to know.

Death, she realized, was something she was getting too equipped at handling.

Past the bathroom, there was a narrow hallway, half-obscured by a steel door. She pushed it open and followed the sound of voices. She knew better than to call out Miranda's name. There were all men speaking, but none of them were Declan or Rope, or even Senator McCormick.

A window. A lab. Miranda on a table, bloodless flesh splayed open like a science class frog. The flowers fell from her hand. Every cell in her body froze cold and hard. She inched her way to the floor, trying not to breathe, trying not to make a sound. She had to get to Rope and the others. She had to warn them, get them out of the house. Did Declan know? Is that why he brought them there, to be experimented on?

She ran upstairs, found Rope and Watch and Preach in the game room playing Tetris. "We have to go," she said. "Now."

"Mouse, what's–"

"They've killed Miranda," she blurted. "They're doing experiments on her. We have to go, now!"

They dropped their controllers. Preach didn't even have shoes on. There was no time to grab bags or jackets. They got downstairs, but Declan was blocking the door. He had a backpack and a pistol.

"Declan, please," Mouse begged. "Please, don't do this. Please just let us go, we won't tell anyone, I swear."

He threw open the door. "C'mon," he said. "We're getting out of here."

‡

Declan took them to his house, another hour from the Senator's, another hour from the lake that had once been their home. "I didn't know," he kept repeating. "I would have never brought you there if I thought…"

Preach cried himself to sleep on the couch. Watch went to

take a shower. Declan left his jacket hanging over a kitchen chair and excused himself to the attic bedroom while Mouse and Rope sat on the stairs, listening to him pace above them. A circle, then down the hallway, halfway down the stairs. Then back up. He let half of "Hungry Like the Wolf" play on the radio before he turned it off.

"What were they doing?" he asked. "To Miranda?"

"It's like they were dissecting her," she said.

"Maybe it was an autopsy," he said. "To find out more about The Hunger?"

"She was alive when we left her," she insisted.

"She lost a lot of blood," he said.

"But why wouldn't they tell us?" she asked. "Why wouldn't they let us say goodbye?"

The footsteps stopped. A door slammed. "I'm going up," said Rope. "Something's not right."

She followed him. The attic suite was sparse; an unfolded pull-out couch, a small TV, a counter with a hot plate and a Mr. Coffee. "Declan?" Mouse called. "Are you okay?"

They heard a snort from the bathroom. They could see one of Declan's Doc Martens through a crack in the door. They pushed inside to see him stretched out in the tub, fully clothed, drinking from a bottle of Wild Turkey. He didn't smile when he saw them. "I'd offer you a drink," he said, taking a pull. "But I'm afraid you're too young."

She didn't like the way he looked at her, like a cartoon coyote eating an oversized steak. No amount of whiskey could dampen that stare.

"I've got it," he finally said. "The Hunger. Probably got it the same time Miranda did. I think my brother put it in the food."

"Why would he do that?" Rope demanded.

Declan laughed. "Because he's an asshole," he said. "Because he needs money for his campaign, and some chemical company was happy to cut a check. A bioweapon. And when their testing proved effective, they flooded the town to cover it all up. He's probably got his hand in that pocket too. They're building a reservoir, you know. Gotta keep those Long Island lawns watered."

So Watch was right. Mouse got so hot with anger she thought she might cook from the inside out. "Is that why you brought us to him?" she hissed. "To experiment on?"

"No," he insisted. "He didn't count on survivors, so he had to pivot. Change the plan. I learned when you did, with Miranda and Charlie. But this variant is stronger. It acts quicker. And it doesn't have to be blood ties. I can feel it inside me. Gnawing. I got halfway down the stairs before I made myself turn back. I thought maybe I could drink it down, smother it, at least for now, but unless I want to stay drunk the rest of my life…."

"Explains why my old man never got it," Rope replied.

Declan didn't laugh. Neither did Mouse. "The files are in my bag," he said, taking another swig. "Everything you need to prove all of this. Go look for yourself if you don't believe me."

She didn't need to see the files. There wasn't time even if she wanted to go take a look. Couldn't risk leaving Rope up here alone. "We'll lock you up until we find a cure," she stammered. "Maybe it will wear off…"

"I know the cure," he said. "It's the pistol in my bag."

"Declan…"

"Don't argue!" he snapped. "I'm almost out of bourbon and the minute I sober up, I'm just going to feel it again. Maybe even stronger than before. Take the other kids and get out. "

She knew he was right. Knew it was the only way. But they

had already lost so much. She wanted to let him devour her. Let the Hunger spread to all of them. Let them feed, for once, surrender to impulse after 17 years of subservience to the adults around her, stop being the good girl she'd always tried to be. She wanted to know what desire felt like in the midst of so much anguish. She wanted to know what it felt like to hunger in a way no food could satiate. Just once.

Rope returned with the pistol and the backpack. He took Declan's keys off the sink. Declan sat up and they shook hands. "Take care of them," he said to both of them. "And when it's safe…tell everyone what my brother did."

She took Declan's coat off the chair. They were getting everyone into the truck when they heard the shot. "What the hell was that?" Watch asked.

Preach didn't need to be told. "God have mercy on his soul," he murmured.

✝

Declan had everything in his backpack. Folders of contracts and lab reports. Miranda's autopsy. Newspaper clippings about the flood and the new reservoir Senator McCormick was proposing. We believe dive teams have recovered the last of the bodies, he'd said from the floor not two days ago. The only thing we can do now is help the survivors heal.

They went back to where they were all first found, on the shores of the lake that used to be their home. They built a shelter of broken car doors and bloated plywood. They built a fire out of broken branches and old magazines. Watch found a plastic bottle of vodka, probably
 washed up from the liquor store, and cracked open the top. "To Declan," he said, taking a swig. "He chose to save us instead of eat us."

The vodka went like fire down Mouse's throat. She felt like a lime slice floating aimlessly in Stephanie's glass a thousand summers ago. Watch and Preach and Rope were all she had left in the world. She couldn't even hold onto the hope that Tonya was still alive. It hurt too much.

She passed the bottle across the fire to Rope. "Let me have some," Preach said.

"It's not communion wine," Rope said. "The blood of Christ or whatever."

"I know," he said. "I just…want to try it."

Rope passed him the bottle. He took a sip, then a drink. "Easy," Watch said, "This stuff will knock you on your ass."

Preach shrugged. "End times are upon us," he said. "Eat, drink, be merry, right?"

Except that there was nothing to eat. No reason to be merry. Nothing but the cold light of day awaiting them. She took another swig when the bottle came back her way. No reason to even wake up at all.

"You think anyone's found him yet?" Watch said.

"What does it matter?" Mouse spat. "He's dead." She didn't know whether to feel sorrow or guilt or betrayal. Maybe it would have been better if she had drowned in the first flood, instead of swallowing all the sorrow that choked her now. She snuggled tighter into Declan's jacket, breathing in the fading traces of his scent, black pepper and sandalwood.

"If Declan got it," Preach said. "And Miranda got it, how do we know we're safe?"

"We don't," Rope said. "All we can do is watch out if one of us starts acting weird."

"And then what?" he asked.

Rope didn't answer.

✣

In the morning, they drove to Albany. Mouse held Declan's backpack in her lap like the nuclear football. Her head hurt. They'd woken up to dampness, a dead fire, and an empty bottle. The ride was silent except for the occasional rumble of someone's stomach or Preach muttering prayers under his breath.

"It'll be okay," she said, putting her hand on his. He was cold. "It'll all be over soon."

Preach smiled at her. He put his head on her shoulder. He smelled like campfire smoke and dirt and the last drink of the night. "I know," he said. "God told me so. Last night."

She couldn't help but laugh. "That might have been the vodka," she joked.

There was a large crowd gathered on the steps of the Capital Plaza. Some of them held up photos of their loved ones. She recognized pictures of her math teacher, a few classmates, her father's boss. There was no one to hold up photos of the three of them. She didn't have a photo of Tonya to wave in the air.

A pastor led them in prayer. A woman sang "Amazing Grace" as a flame was passed through the crowd, sparking white taper candles in milky plastic cups. Mouse held hers close, letting the flame warm her face. For her father. For Stephanie. For the memory of Tonya, wherever she was.

"I mourn with you," said Senator McCormick as he took the podium. "Not just for the friends and loved ones you have lost, but also for the brother I lost yesterday, Declan McCormick."

"That son of a bitch," Rope muttered.

"We must all work together to remember," he said. "To rebuild. To honor those whose lives were cut too short, too soon."

Rope nodded to Watch. It was time. Now or never. "Senator

McCormick is lying!" Watch shouted. "He allowed Truce to be flooded to cover up for testing a bioweapon!"

Senator John froze at the podium. He covered the microphone with his hand, whispered something to his aides. "Those allegations are false, defamatory, and despicable," he said when he turned back. "These people are here to mourn, not to push tabloid fantasies."

But all eyes were on them now. "We have the paperwork," Watch continued. "From Declan, before he killed himself after you infected him. Including the autopsy of our friend Miranda Fisher. You killed her too, after you dosed her and let her eat her baby. For what, Senator! Campaign contributions?"

Preach stepped forward. "Preach, come back here," Rope murmured. "It's not time yet."

"Let him go," Watch said. "He knows what he's doing."

A security officer stepped out in front of him when he reached the stage. "Step back," he ordered.

Mouse knew what was coming.

Preach obeyed. Then, like a bullet, he leapt onto the security officer, tearing bloody flesh in his teeth. There were screams and gunshots. The fleeing crowd was another flood around her. This time she couldn't move, couldn't ride the waves to safety. She was frozen to the ground no matter how hard Rope tugged on her sleeve. She couldn't take her eyes off Preach, blood-soaked and wild. How long had he held the Hunger inside him? Was that the chill she felt in his hands, the prayers whispered for strength to hold out just a little while longer?

There was nowhere for Senator McCormick to flee from the stage. The crowds were pulling away too fast for him to get a foothold and not be trampled. His own monster was advancing towards him. There was a scream, another gunshot, and then nothing.

Maybe in the morning the newspapers would lead with Senator John's murder at the hands of a crazed lunatic. Or maybe the papers would publish the story of what really happened. In death, she hoped, he wouldn't be able to hide from his crimes. Someone would have to pay for the blood that had been shed.

Mouse thought she heard someone shriek her name across the now-empty plaza. She turned and saw no one. She heard it again, closer, until she turned around and saw Watch and Rope. Watch still had the backpack. Rope held Tonya in his arms. She ran to them, scooping up her sister, breathing in the baby-soft scent of her neck as she squeaked her sister's name. She vowed to never be apart from her again.

"Where was she?" she gasped. "Oh Tonya, I've missed you so much!"

"By the fountain," Rope said. "Whoever she was with must have run off. C'mon, we've gotta get out of here."

There would be time to hear her sister's story later. How she floated downstream like Baby Moses. How someone rescued her, only to dump her when the chaos broke out. It didn't matter. They were together again. The four of them could figure out a way to be a family, to make up for everything they'd lost. Wherever they landed, they'd be together.

Mouse's own stomach rumbled. "You must be starving," she said, brushing back her sister's hair. "Let's get something to eat."

Libby Cudmore is the author of *Negative Girl* (Datura 2024) and *The Big Rewind* (William Morrow 2016) as well as the Wade & Jacks series at *Ellery Queen Mystery Magazine, Tough* and *Alfred Hitchcock's Mystery Magazine*. She has also been published in *The Dark, Bleed Error, Smokelong Quarterly, Had, Monkeybicycle, Orca,* and others. She is also a four-year alumni of the Barrelhouse Writer Camp, the recipient of the 2023 Black Orchid Novella Award, the 2023 Shamus Award for Best Short Story and the 2018 Oregon Writer's Colony prize.

THE SEA IS FULL OF GHOSTS

Dannye Chase

"I think you were meant to move on," the merman says. He means it as a kindness.

He's not sure the sailor can grasp what he's saying. The sea is deep here, and sound travels well, but he's guessing on the language based on the ragged strips of flag that wave limply with the current, and he's not very fluent in human tongues anyway.

The merman has been told the sea is full of ghosts, but this is the first he's found. It seems horribly cruel for a sailor to be alone in the ocean on a fractured ship that's being devoured by creatures he never knew existed.

Humans hung their afterlife in the clouds. It bothers the merman that the man might believe this place is Hell.

The sailor doesn't give much attention to the sunken ship he stands on, always gazing into the distance. But it's so dark the merman wonders if the sailor is seeing dreams instead of depths. Does he think he's on the surface? Does he think the sky is blue?

The merman hasn't been alive so long that he remembers huge wooden ships like this one, but he's seen humans glide above him on wood and metal, plastic, foam, anything that will float. Humans don't belong on the sea, but they don't seem to understand that, so they keep coming, and they keep sinking. Sometimes they die in dry clothes and their bodies are tossed overboard. Sometimes the whole ship comes down.

This ship broke apart before it sank. Pieces of it are scattered on the seafloor, carelessly dropped. The sailor stands on the largest expanse of deck that still exists. He walks it sometimes, around the edges that stab sharply at the sea but cause it no harm. He couldn't have sailed the ship himself. There had to have been many other men. But he is the only one here. Perhaps the sailor is in Hell, the merman thinks. Perhaps he has been damned. If so, what does that make the merman?

The merman once swore to himself he would never descend to this depth. He isn't sure if he talks to the sailor because he doesn't want to be alone in this place or because he's trying to convince himself he is alone, that the ghost is a ghost and can therefore be ignored, that there's no more sentience in him than the ship under his feet. He's just something that happened.

"I think you were meant to move on," the merman says, nearly every day. The sailor makes no sign of having heard or seen him, though the merman is easily visible down here with his white scales. The merman keeps himself white because it's pretty and attracts fish, and when he moves quickly, it confuses the bigger things that lurk in the dark. As far as the merman can tell, he is the only creature that's noticed the sailor. The bigger things don't try to eat him, visible as he is with his pale skin and shirt.

The sailor's expression changes sometimes. He looks pained or sad, lonely, frightened. Once the merman saw him smile and it chilled him even in the deep sea. What was the sailor smiling at? A memory? Or could he actually see something in these waters that was invisible to the merman?

Is the sailor not the only ghost down here, but rather the only one pale enough to see?

The merman swims large circles around the ruined ship at first, but later he comes up to the railing, to the spongy deck itself. "What will you do when your ship disappears?" he asks. There never comes an answer. So the merman tells the sailor what he's done during the day, what he ate, what tried to eat him. He speaks about his nearly-forgotten family and friends, the pet anglerfish he had as a child that he misses more than anyone else.

He tells the sailor it's cold here on the seafloor, that it's dark, and what it feels like when your body is compressed by the weight of the water. How the other merpeople don't come down here because it's hard to breathe. How it makes him feel like he's dying and at the same time like he's fighting to live.

"Your body is long gone," the merman says. He means it as a kindness. He hopes the sailor can't feel the cold or pressure. The merman would have eaten the body if he'd found it, but he leaves this part out. He's not sure why, because when the merman dies— or maybe before—something will certainly eat him.

The merman never gives the sailor a name. He doesn't want him to turn his head at the sound of it. But the merman does start to make up stories, as if to comfort him. "You were a captain. The rest were rescued, but you stayed on your ship until the end. You won't leave it even now."

The merman spins a tale: the sailor has a family who misses him and remembers him on holidays. He had a lover aboard his ship who escaped, and ever afterward the broken-hearted man stared at the sea, remembering his brave captain. But the merman also says the sailor has broken things that can't be repaired, because if the rest is fantasy, surely that is real.

But when he says this, the sailor smiles again, and it is not a pretty smile. There is a cruel pleasure to it, in the show of teeth and the thinning of lips, and the merman has never been afraid of what horrible wonders are down here, but he is now.

The merman never goes back. He thinks guilt is easier to stomach than ghosts.

Dannye Chase is a queer, married mom of three who lives in the US Pacific Northwest. She claims to write in many genres, but her oldest offspring suspects it all boils down to either romance or horror...or somehow both. Dannye's short fiction has or will appear on the podcast No Sleep, the anthology *Anna Karenina Isn't Dead* from Improbable Press, and Allegory and Nocturne magazines. You can find her on Twitter as Dannye Chase, and at DannyeChase.com, where she gives weird writing prompts.

Cruel To Be Kind

Jacqueline Freimor

The summer of your junior year, the heat and humidity broke records, and just your luck, that was the summer you'd decided to stay in town to take a few classes. Because only the library and some of the local restaurants were air-conditioned, you spent most days in stifling classrooms sweating through your clothes, the air a hot, damp hand clamped over your nose and mouth. You spent most nights slapping at no-see-ums in an apartment the temperature of blood.

After class on the worst days, your friend would take you to Little Creek Falls, a swimming hole only the locals knew. She'd park and the two of you would launch yourselves from the car, plunge into the icy water, and splash up to the surface, gasping, then sun yourselves on the flat rocks like lizards. She brought the boombox and you brought the food. You lay back, popping frozen grapes in your mouth while listening to The Pretenders. Blondie. Nick Lowe.

Your friend was both Town and Gown because her father was a professor at the law school, but she also attended the university. As such, her allegiances were murky. She was a tennis player, an A student, a girl whose ancestors were landed gentry, but she was also a drinker, a party girl, a girl who knew all the dealers and had slept with most of them, too.

"Don't look now," she said one day at the Falls, "but there's the guy I told you about." On the radio, Chrissie Hynde was singing about getting people's attention.

You cracked your eyes open and saw her raise her chin the tiniest bit. "Which guy?"

"The one who gave me crabs."

You followed the line of her jaw and saw him a few rocks over, sharing a joint with two other guys. "Oh, right," you said. "Ugh."

"Just wanted to warn you," she said.

"Thanks," you said, "but he's not my type." Actually, you
were probably not his type, even though singing and playing guitar
at night in the local bars had earned you a little social capital.
Mostly you were an A student, like her, but awkward with it, a
scholarship kid, a northerner, whose ancestral roots ran only as
deep as the Jewish Diaspora of Eastern Europe.

"What would you do without me?" she said, smiling, and
closed her eyes. She wasn't beautiful, but she had silky white-
blonde hair and an easy laugh. She was the coolest person you
knew. You were probably a little in love with her.

A few days later, you did meet your type at a Lost Dogs gig at
the Outpost, when he spotted you dancing in the hot, seething
crowd and asked if you wanted to get high with the band. You did;
you absolutely did. He wasn't a student, he was a short-order cook
and part-time dealer, and he liked musicians, so you went home
with him that night and most nights after that. Sometimes you slept
in his room and sometimes you lay on a blanket on the roof,
tripping, watching bats take flight across the purpling sky. Your
sweating bodies fit like jigsaw pieces, he said, his hand twisted in
your hair.

You thought about introducing them, your friend and your
boyfriend, but couldn't seem to get around to it, which was
probably just as well. She was good but wanted to be bad, and he
was bad but wanted to be good, and you were, face it, worried that
if they met, they might decide to split the difference. It didn't help
that you didn't know if you were good or bad or even what you
wanted most of the time.

The one thing you knew for sure: you wanted him, the
longing a constant sharp pain like a knife between your ribs. Even
after he told you over breakfast one morning that, by the way, he

had herpes, but it was no big deal, he'd had it for years.

You set your coffee mug down carefully, trying to hide your dismay and calculating the number of times you'd had sex without a condom. "Why didn't you tell me?" you finally said.

He shrugged. "Like I said, it's no big deal. I'm only contagious when I'm having an outbreak, and I always know when that is." He laughed. "You should see your face. Relax! Do you really think I'd do anything to hurt you?"

"No," you said, "I know you wouldn't," but Debbie Harry was singing in your head about how fragile love was, how breakable.

He beckoned with an eggy fork. "Get over here. Let me show you how crazy I am about you."

And you went.

Humiliating.

Also humiliating: confessing to the doctor at Student Health. She was a kind woman. She took your blood painlessly and then examined you as you lay knees up, feet in stirrups, staring at the poster of Monet's "Water Lilies" tacked to the ceiling, while she told you not to worry, worrying never changed anything, she didn't see any lesions but she'd have your lab results in two weeks and you'd take it from there.

Two weeks.

You didn't know what to do, whether to break up with him or just roll with it because you loved him, and love wasn't all rainbows and unicorns, you weren't stupid, you weren't a child. Besides, your friend would have let it slide. She hadn't freaked out when she caught crabs, just bagged her mattress in plastic and washed her clothes, although sometimes when you were in her apartment, you wondered if any of the bugs were still there, lurking deep in the couch.

To buy yourself time to decide, you phoned him and said you had to stay home for a couple of days to study for midterms, then called the friend you'd been neglecting. When she answered, she said, "Who is this?" as nastily as possible, but you apologized all over yourself, you were so, so sorry, and hand to God it would never happen again, so she softened and invited you over to watch Hill Street Blues.

During the first commercial she went to the fridge and you told her what had happened.

"Shit," she said, pulling two ice pops from the freezer. She tossed one across the room. "Do you love him?"

You managed to catch it and held it to your forehead and the back of your neck. "Yeah," you said. "It's only been a few days, and I miss him already." A tear rolled down your cheek, hot and fat, your head was swollen with pain that seeped from your eyes like pus. You tore at the plastic wrap. The orange ice was so cold it burned.

Leaning on the fridge, she peeled her ice pop, bit off a piece, and chewed. She pointed the stick at the phone sitting on the coffee table.

"Really?" you said.

She shrugged. "That's what I would do," she said, enunciating carefully around a mouthful of slush. "If I loved him. Duh."

Immediately you knew she was right, you were an idiot, you were making everything too complicated. You missed lying on the grass with him, watching the scudding clouds, you missed kissing the ropy veins snaking up his arms, you missed breathing in the smoky smell of his skin. So you would call him. You'd tell him you'd see him in a couple of days.

You wiped your tears, shifted yourself across the couch, and dialed. Your heart was dancing in your chest.

On the third ring a woman said, "Hello?"

You blinked hard, then asked for your boyfriend.

"Hold on, I'll get him," the woman said. She put the phone down and you heard voices laughing, shrieking, Led Zeppelin's "Whole Lotta Love" blasting from the stereo. You held out the receiver so your friend could hear, and she slitted her eyes and cocked her head.

"Hello?" your boyfriend said.

You jammed the phone up against your ear. "Hey, it's me."

A beat. "Oh, hey! How you doing?"

"Good. So, are you, like, throwing a party?" You were staring at your friend.

Another beat. "Not really. Just having some people over."

The bottom fell out of your stomach. "And you didn't invite me?"

"Well, uh…it's raining."

"It's raining?"

"Yeah. I was going to call, but it started raining. I know you don't like walking in the rain."

You were going to be sick. Something sticky was dripping down your hand. You looked at it, at the orange sugar water puddling on the table, then looked up at your friend.

"Hang up," she said.

"I don't…I don't know what to say," you told your boyfriend.

"Hang up," your friend said louder.

"Listen," your boyfriend said. "I think we need to talk."

"Hang it the fuck up!" your friend yelled. She ran across the room, grabbed the receiver, and slammed it down in its cradle. "Damn it, girl! What's wrong with you?"

You didn't know. But you suspected it was that you just

weren't good enough.

‡

A week later, you were on break between sets at Miz Annie's, your Friday gig, and of course the a/c was broken, so your hands were sweaty, they had been slipping off the guitar strings all night. Your friend was drinking one of your two free beers. You'd already chugged yours—probably not a good idea. You'd had a few at home before you left.

"Look," your friend said for the tenth time, "just get back on the horse. There are a lot of guys in the world." She scanned the dim bar and flicked her eyes. "What about him?"

The guy's face was tinted red, then blue, then green under the Christmas lights no one had bothered to take down. "No," you said. "Too curly." Meaning too Jewish, but you couldn't say that to a non-Jew.

"You're curly," she said.

"Be that as it may. Next."

Her delicate nostrils flared. "Why are you being such a gigantic pain in the ass?"

"Thank you. That's helpful."

"That's tough love, my friend. Because I care about you." She sang the chorus of Nick Lowe's "Cruel to Be Kind."

She was singing completely out of tune, which gave you a kind of savage satisfaction. "Seriously," you said, "I think he's sleeping with Cassie. Do you think he's sleeping with Cassie?" Cassie was a musician who looked like Stevie Nicks but sang in a surprisingly deep and soulful voice. You'd wanted to hate Cassie but couldn't, she'd been nothing but sweet to you.

Your friend shrugged. "Maybe. Does it matter?"

You punched her in the shoulder harder than you intended. "Of course it matters."

"Hey!" she said, rubbing her upper arm.

"Sorry." But you weren't.

She flashed you an angry glance. "God, cut it out already. Who he's sleeping with is none of your business anymore. The only thing that matters is he's not sleeping with you."

It felt like a slap. Your face even tingled. You'd thought after a full week of crying you were all cried out, but surprise, surprise, you were wrong. The tears stung like acid.

Mortifying.

"Why don't you just go," you said. Your voice was thin and strained, escaping from your strangled throat.

She stood. Hesitated. "I didn't mean—"

"Leave me alone, okay?"

She stared at you for a moment, then shrugged and turned her back. The plastic strips tied to the box fan on the bar waved her out the door.

You watched her go, then saw the bartender give you the high sign; your break was over. You passed a napkin across your face, shuddered a few breaths, and chugged the rest of her beer before hitting the stage.

Your beer. It was your beer.

‡

By the time you came to class the next morning, you knew you'd been a jerk, but your friend ignored you every time you tried to catch her eye. Now she had left you, too, and you had nobody. You wanted to die. You were the world's biggest loser.

You hurried to catch up with her afterward. "Can we talk?" you said, and she stopped walking to face you.

"Fine," she said. "Talk."

"I'm sorry, I'm so sorry. I know I've been a really, really bad friend, really self-pitying and self-absorbed. I know you were just trying to help.”

She gripped her textbook to her chest, keeping a barrier between you, but you saw that she was listening.

“Also, I was drunk off my ass,” you continued. “Not an excuse—I’m just trying to explain. Anyway, they fired me. Miz Annie’s.”

And then she was your friend again. Her brow wrinkled with concern. “No way! What happened?”

You shook your head. You’d been so trashed, you could remember the night only in horror-filled flashes. You did remember that your fingers didn’t work right and you slurred your way through the songs, and when someone in the audience heckled you, you called him an asshole. Then your guitar string broke, and you actually cried and tried to change it in the middle of your set, and you pricked a couple of fingers and when you saw that you were bleeding you cried some more, and it was maybe then that you started babbling about your ex-boyfriend and the bouncer and bartender dragged you off stage and out the door. You didn’t remember how you got home. Only the thin smear of blood on your pillow in the morning convinced you it hadn’t been a nightmare.

Now you told her all of it, every sickening detail, the swampy air encircling you like a python. You told her she didn’t have to worry, you were done wallowing, and she hugged you. Then the two of you went to Little Creek Falls, where even though you were Jewish, you baptized yourself and were reborn.

Clean.

‡

After that, you expected to run into your ex-boyfriend everywhere, and when you didn’t, you realized how quickly you had entered his world but that he'd never entered yours at all. With the extra time on your hands, you reacquainted yourself with your books and hung out with your friend and when the doctor at Student Health called to tell you your test results were negative, you were relieved, of course, you told yourself, yes-siree-bob, you'd really dodged a bullet there. You tried to be happy, you told yourself you were happy.

The heat and humidity were unrelenting. One day you and your friend left the classroom wringing wet and stood outside Dawson Hall plucking your tank tops away from your slick skin, trying to catch a breeze. It was a perfect day for the Falls. You wanted to submerge yourself in the freezing water and not surface until October.

You waited for her to suggest a trip and were surprised when she didn't. You dropped hints—wow, it was really hot today, wasn't it, maybe the hottest day yet—and still she said nothing. You didn't feel you could ask outright, it was her car after all, and her gas, even though she laughed every time you suggested you give her gas money. So you asked what she was doing the rest of the afternoon.

"I have to go to the club with my parents," she said awkwardly.

She was usually so down-to-earth you kept forgetting how rich her family was, and then she'd say something about "the club" and it would jolt you every time, you'd have to shift your frame of reference. "Oh, no," you said, "not with the parents," and mimed a shiver. "Is there a party there or something?"

Her eyes slid away from yours. "Um, yeah, a pool party. It's for members," she added.

Well, duh, you wanted to say, of course clubs had events for members, but in your experience clubs usually let their members bring guests. "Is it a nice pool?" you said, still angling for an invitation. "Nicer than Little Creek Falls?" It was so damn hot, and you didn't want to have to sit in the library the whole afternoon. Or go home and stand in a cold shower, then lie spreadeagled on your bed willing yourself not to sweat.

"Yeah," she said, shifting her weight. "The pool is great. But the club members are kind of…conservative. We'll go to the Falls tomorrow, okay? Promise."

Confused, you watched as a flush slowly rose from her chest all the way up to her white-blonde hairline. You'd never seen her blush before, fair as she was, you were the blusher, always balanced on a knife-edge over a flaming pit of embarrassment. "Sure," you finally managed to say.

She squeezed your arm. "See you."

"See you," you echoed. "Have fun."

‡

It took you hours to figure out what had happened, hours of probing your discomfort like a decaying tooth, until you realized the only possible reason she hadn't invited you to the club was so simple, so obvious, you were angry with yourself you hadn't seen it right away.

Conservative, she'd said. And here you were, so used to thinking of yourself as an American you sometimes forgot you were a Jew. Good enough for the Falls, but not good enough for the club.

You saw her the next day, another scorcher, and when neither of you mentioned the pool party, you knew something in your relationship had shifted, your friendship was a boat that had slipped its moorings, its ties less secure than you'd thought. She took you to the Falls, but everything was spoiled now, green-brown slime coating the rocks, clouds of gnats swarming the water, a bloated fish floating belly up. On the radio, someone was singing about heartache, so when some dealer your friend knew asked if you wanted to drop acid, you plucked the tab from his hand and jammed it under your tongue like a thermometer, like it could tell you what was wrong with you. Before too long you felt yourself flush with fever, you were glowing from within, a furnace was burning under your skin.

Don't look at the sun, stupid, your friend said, so you looked at her instead but she was melting, her chin stretching down, her flesh thinning and slipping to the ground, you could see her skull.

You screamed without a sound because your heart was pumping in your throat and she touched your cheek and said, Oh, no, her tinny voice playing through the Victrola rising into the air from the scummy pool. Look at me. It's me. It's just me.

You looked at her hard and she was herself again, there was her pale skin, there were her blue eyes. I'm scared, you said.

I know, she said, let's go, and you were sitting in the grass by the Science Building, firefly trails in the night sky were spelling out what you had to do, and you wanted to write it all down, if only you could write it all down. A giant black dog trotted over, he said he was thirsty, so you found a drawer and filled it with water. Then you were sitting on a wall, legs dangling, and you studied your friend's face, afraid it would change again, and twice it did but each time she helped you stop it before it got really bad.

At four in the morning you were both eating pancakes at Frank's All-Nite Diner, and you knew you were coming down from the acid because you knew that it was four o'clock and that you were eating pancakes. They tasted raw, though, they were disgusting. You didn't send them back because maybe you were wrong.

She drove you home. You slept for twelve hours, missing all

your classes.

‡

After that, your friend didn't say anything about what had
happened that day and neither did you, you were ashamed of
having been so needy, so weak, there was so much about yourself
you wanted to apologize for that you didn't know where to start.
You still went with her to the Falls when she suggested it, you
pretended everything was normal, but it was not; it really was not.
It was hotter than ever and every day felt wrong to you, you were a
swollen door that didn't fit its frame.

You knew your friend's feelings about you had changed, even
though she didn't show it. There she was taking notes in class,
there she was driving with one hand on the wheel, she was talking,
she was smiling, she was laughing, but you sensed her love for you
had peeled off her heart, she'd shed it like snakeskin. The next
time you went to the Falls you saw it dive into the pool after her, a
murky shadow, but you blinked, and when you looked again it was
gone. Sorrow welled in you then, ballooning behind your eyes.

She bobbed to the surface and started treading water, heat
shimmers warping the air above her hair. "What's the matter?" she
said.

You wanted to tell her, to beg her to let you back into her life,
you couldn't lose her, too, but you knew she would tell you she
didn't know what you were talking about and to stop being
dramatic.

"I was just thinking about my guitar strings," you said
inanely, which you hadn't been at all, but as soon as you said it
you remembered that the day before, your high e had broken and
when you'd stuffed it into the case with the other busted strings
you'd never thrown out, you'd been paralyzed by the idea, by the
utter clarity of the idea, that they were the strings of your psyche,

once taut and gleaming, until the twist of a peg had been one twist too many.

She rolled her eyes. "Okay, crazy," she said, then sank below the surface.

Maybe that's what was the matter.

Maybe you were crazy.

‡

A few days later you woke after a fitful night, the hot, damp sheets twisted around your torso like a straitjacket. Juddering in your mind's eye was your boyfriend's favorite T-shirt, the faded green T-shirt with the Lucky Charms leprechaun clicking his heels and waving a wand over the words *magically delicious!*, it was the shirt he'd been wearing the night you met and he'd said exactly that after kissing you, he'd said, "Magically delicious," and you'd laughed.

The memory chewed at the edge of your consciousness all day, it was tearing at your brain with its tiny razor teeth. It wouldn't stop, you didn't know why, until that night at your gig at No-Name Bar, your boyfriend showed up in the middle of your set and he was wearing that shirt, the very same Lucky Charms T-shirt, it was like you had conjured him up, it was an omen. You faltered for a moment but then got it together, you were doing okay, your voice sounded good and for once your fingers were limber and dry, gliding nimbly over the strings.

Your boyfriend crossed the room and said something to the bartender, and when she handed him a bottle he turned to lean against the bar, long legs crossed at the ankle, watching you. You were singing Elton John's song about how hard it was to apologize and you were singing to him, you were singing to yourself. When he raised his beer in a salute, you smiled. You thought, Maybe…?

Then you saw the door open and your friend came in, caught

your eye, thumbs up. You saw her go to the bar, you saw him see her and her see him, and you knew what was going to happen, it was inevitable. She ordered a drink and he straightened up and turned away from you, he turned to her, and then they were talking, she was facing out, elbows behind her on the bar top, one heel hooked on the foot rail. She tossed her head, white-blonde hair rippling.

In an instant you were an electrical storm of rage, you were sure your curls were standing on end, crackling and hissing, lightning shooting from your mouth. Somehow you finished the song, hitting the wrong final chord and quickly correcting it, but it was too late, the dissonance hung in the air like poison gas. The audience might have clapped; you didn't know. You told them you'd be back after a break, plunked down your guitar, and made for the bar. He was gone by the time you got there.

"Where'd he go?" you said to your friend.

"Who?" she said. "And hi. You sounded great." She looked fresh and cool. Her teeth gleamed in the dim light.

"You know. The guy you were talking to."

She half-turned to put her bottle on the bar and turned back. "Bathroom. He's cute."

You felt a vein pulse in your forehead. "You know who he is, right?"

She peered at you, then her eyes widened. "Oh."

You couldn't believe that was all she could say, Oh. You waited for her to go on but she didn't. Oh, it was like she didn't know how you felt, it was like she didn't know you. You moved your face close to hers, close enough to bite her.

She laughed her easy laugh but still leaned away from you. "What."

"Don't fuck my boyfriend," you said, enunciating each word.

Her expression changed then. She was calculating her response, you could see through her skull to the abacus of her brain, you could hear the balls click as she pushed them first one way, then the other. "I didn't know it was him."

"Well now you do. So don't."

She snorted in derision. "That's not up to you, is it? I mean, he's not your boyfriend anymore."

It was like she'd kicked you in the stomach, all the air left your lungs, you couldn't talk, you couldn't breathe. After a moment, you felt your lips pull back in a rictus of a smile, you tried to stop them but couldn't. "Are you kidding me?"

She shrugged. "Anyway, we were just talking," she said. "Lighten up."

You grabbed her wrists and squeezed. "Promise me."

"Let go," she said and tried to twist away, but you tightened your grip. You saw the surprise in her eyes change to fear, she hadn't known how strong your hands were, how years and years of practicing guitar scales had turned your hands into manacles.

"Say it," you said.

"Fine, I promise," she said and you released her. She massaged one wrist, then the other and glared at you. "That really hurt."

"I'm sorry," you said, the words sounding insincere even to yourself.

"You're a psycho, you know that?" she said. You could see that under the bluster she was still afraid.

That was okay with you, if her fear kept her away from your boyfriend, which it did. You were on stage when he returned to the bar, and although he and your friend chatted for a few minutes, you were triumphant when you saw her drift away and drape herself all over some other guy. After a while, your boyfriend left, and then your friend left with her one-night stand.

You left at two o'clock after your last set, but you didn't go home; somehow you found yourself across the street from your boyfriend's apartment building, standing behind a tree, looking up at the shade in his window, watching his silhouette move back and forth across the room. After a while the light went out, but you could still see him, the shape of him, when you closed your eyes.

‡

The next morning your friend started avoiding you, coming in late to class so she wouldn't have to sit next to you and hurrying out as soon as class was over. You were devastated at first. Every time you saw her it felt like someone was clawing your chest open and digging for your heart, but then you made yourself remember her treachery at the bar, you remembered how when you were tripping you saw the flesh melting off her bones, it was the drug's way of revealing the truth of what she was, the truth that she was a monster.

The heat in your apartment made it impossible to sleep, so you returned to the tree across from your boyfriend's building every night, even after your gigs, and kept watch until his light went out, every night the sweat beading at your hairline and on your upper lip and at the hollow of your throat, the wet air sticking to your skin like plastic wrap, the mosquitoes whining and crickets sharpening their wings like knives. Once your boyfriend left his apartment late and you followed him to Miz Annie's, you were sure he was meeting someone there. The whole time you were waiting, you felt like you'd been flayed alive, you were a writhing mass of bleeding tissue, until he finally left the bar and you saw that he was alone.

After more than a week of watching him come home alone you started to wonder why. Could it be that when he'd seen you at

No-Name Bar, he'd realized just how much he still loved you? It was possible, you realized, in fact, it was likely, so you stopped going to his building at night and waited for him to call you. You weren't going to call him; you had your pride. You were good enough, you were more than good enough. He'd helped you see that. He'd broken up with you to teach you a lesson, to make you stronger, he'd been using tough love, just like the song said, just like your friend said.

You didn't want to leave your apartment. You had to be there when your boyfriend called, so you canceled your gigs and stopped going to class, even though finals were coming up and you'd probably fail and lose your scholarship. Night followed day followed night, you lost track, the air was so swampy you could barely sleep, you could barely eat, everything you put in your mouth tasted like soot. You started taking the phone with you when you moved around the apartment, you stretched the cord as far as it would go, you stared at the phone and concentrated on making it ring the way you'd made your boyfriend appear at No-Name Bar in his Lucky Charms T-shirt. Once you were sure it was ringing, but when you picked up the receiver and whispered, Hello?, your voice thin and dusty with disuse, there was nothing, only a dial tone. You hummed along with it for a while, harmonizing with the pitches, maybe you could send a message to your boyfriend through the wires, but then you realized he was probably trying to call that very minute and getting a busy signal. Panicked, you hung up, listening, the phone was silent, or wait—was it ringing? You picked up the receiver again and again, but there was so much static in your ears, so much crackling and scratching, you couldn't tell if he was on the line.

Finally you slammed the phone down and jumped to your feet, you had to know, you had to find out what was going on, you ran out of the apartment and back to the tree across the street from your boyfriend's window. The shade was up but the room was dark, so you checked your watch; still early. You envisioned him coming home, alone as usual, you saw yourself stepping out from the shadows and saying his name, you saw him turn, his face breaking into a dazzling smile, you knew then you'd been wrong to leave it up to him, you knew he'd been waiting for you all along, waiting for you to make the first move. The universe knew it, too. The air held its hot breath. All the insects were still.

You didn't know how long you stood there, eyes closed, watching your reunion advance frame by frame in the slide projector in your head. Click-click slide-click, you heard, click-click slide-click, over the vibrating motor, each jerk of the carousel bringing him closer and closer. Click-click slide-click. Click-click slide-click.

The sound of a different motor drowned out the projector, you opened your eyes to see a silver Mercedes pulling gracefully to the curb in front of your boyfriend's building. You saw your boyfriend appear on the sidewalk, unfurling himself from the car and rising to his full height like a flower, it was a magic trick, you were so riveted by the sight that you didn't see your friend at first, her hair in a gleaming French twist, sitting behind the driver, an older man with the same exact profile as hers, they were two perfect cameos. You watched in disbelief as your boyfriend closed his door with a thunk and put his hands on the roof, leaning down and out of your view. You heard a chorus of farewells, laughter, two men's voices, two women's voices, and your boyfriend straightened up and waved as the car purred away. He was wearing a suit and tie and dress shoes. You hadn't known he even owned clothes like that. Fancy clothes. Clothes you'd need if you were, say, going to a party at a country club.

For a long time you sat in the dirt behind the tree, rocking back and forth, hands pressed to your mouth. It was long enough for him to go inside, to parade across the shade, to turn out the light. Long enough for you to plan what you had to do.

‡

You arrived at your friend's apartment early the next morning, there were no classes, she'd be home, she was always home and awake on Saturday mornings. When she opened the door, all crisp and clean in her sundress and sandals, she stared at you in shock, you saw anger, and pity, and sadness, and also disgust in her blue eyes, you saw it all in an instant and you saw what she saw, you were gaunt, haggard, your unwashed clothes hanging off your frame, your hair frizzed out like a dandelion puffball, like a weed, like an ugly, invasive, unwanted weed.

"Oh my God," she said. "What happened to you?"

Her face was creased with concern, her voice so kind you wanted to cry, for a split second you wanted to sink into her arms and tell her everything, she was your friend, she was your beautiful friend, she loved you, she would help you. Then you remembered what really lived inside her, what she had done to you, what she was doing to you, and you heard Tom Petty singing, "Fooled Again," so you told yourself to act weak, she liked you weak, you couldn't let her know how strong you really were.

"It's a long story," you said, letting the corners of your mouth turn down. "Can I come in?"

As sorry as she was for you, she was also wary, you could see it in the way she leaned against the door jamb, blocking your entry. "I don't know," she said. "I'm still upset about what you did to me at the bar. You hurt me."

"I know," you said. "I can't apologize enough. I was…I was acting crazy, just like you said. But I'm better now."

She looked skeptical, and you realized you were going at this the wrong way, she wanted you to need her, she wanted you to beg.

"Please," you said desperately. "I'm so sorry, I know what I did was bad, I can't tell you how sorry I am. I'll keep saying it for months, for years if I have to, I'll do anything it takes to get you to trust me again. Please. I miss you. I really, really miss you."

Your desperation was real, it wasn't put on, not because you wanted to be friends again but because you didn't have months, you didn't have years. Because you couldn't wait that long to be reunited with your boyfriend.

Your boyfriend. He was your boyfriend.

You fingered the guitar strings in your pocket, all the busted strings you had found in your guitar case the night before and had twisted and braided and twisted again in an unbreakable loop, a loop that could be pulled tight around the neck by somebody with strong hands. Hands like manacles.

"Okay," she said, a hint of smugness in her tone. "I'll help you get cleaned up."

She stepped back.

She let you in.

Jacqueline Freimor won first prize in the Unpublished Writers category of the MWA's 50th Anniversary Short Story Competition in 1995, which included publication in *Alfred Hitchcock Mystery Magazine*. Since then, her stories have appeared in Ellery Queen Mystery Magazine, Rock and a Hard Place Magazine, Vautrin, Black Cat Weekly, and Mystery Magazine, among others. She has also been reprinted in *The Best Mystery Stories of the Year: 2021*, *The Best American Mystery and Suspense 2022*, and *The Best American Mystery and Suspense 2023*. Her novella *The Case of the Bogus Cinderellas*, which won the 2022 Black Orchid Novella Award, was published in the July/August 2023 issue of Alfred Hitchcock Mystery Magazine.

Acknowledgments

We owe our sincere thanks to our listeners, as well as our previous guests, as we would not be here without you. Beyond that, we would like to extend our thanks to Rijk van Zanten, Rhiannon Petras, Bobby Mathews, James and Brianna Turner, and John Herrmann. You're all wonderful people and we're forever grateful for your support.

About Dark Waters

Dark Waters is a literary podcast started in 2021 focused on dark fiction and those to love and read and write it. The show embraces authors from all manners of dark fiction, from crime to horror to cozies and everything in between. The show published its first anthology of in 2023, *Dark Waters vol. 1.* You can find more information at https://linktr.ee/darkwaterspod, or follow the podcast on Bluesky, Twitter, and Instagram to stay up to date on new episodes.

About our editors:

Kirstyn Petras is a Brooklyn-based fiction writer but primarily identifies as caffeine in a human suit held together by hair spray and sheer force of will. Her short stories have been published in Punk Noir, Hoosier Noir, Metastellar, and A Thin Slice of Anxiety. Her debut novel, *The Next Witness,* was the winner of the 2023 NYC Big Book Award for Political Thriller. When not writing, she trains contortion and aerial hoop, and uses chasing her cats as cardio.

N.B. Turner is a writer living in Nebraska, remembering and trying to honor his time growing up along the Great Lakes. He's published short fiction in Hoosier Noir, Shotgun Honey, Pulp Modern Flash, Expat Lit, Punk Noir and Rock and A Hard Place Magazine, as well as poetry in The Daily Drunk and Punk Noir. He is also the editor of Hoosier Noir.

Trigger Warnings

This is a collection of dark fiction stories, and as such, readers should expect stories with darkness in them, including, but not limited to, violence, manipulation, death, suffering, murder, assault, and bigotry.

Outside of that, there are a few extra triggers listed here, for readers who wish to be aware of such content.

Road Work: Sexual Assault

Animal Remains, We Hunger: Violence against children

The Bunker: Violence relating to war

Mad Mara, Avoiding the Holes: Violence in a medical setting

Vacationland: Violence against women

Cruel to be Kind: Stalking